G. Keller

Roach Girl origin trilogy one

G. Keller

Mileyjackmedia

Orlando, Florida

G. Keller

Roach Girl origin trilogy one
Mileyjackmedia, LLC
Orlando, Florida

ISBN 979-8-9994287-0-7

This story was printed in the United States of America.

Cover Art by Janelle Bell-Martin

My deepest thanks to God for the strength, courage, and perseverance to create this trilogy.

G. Keller

"I learned this, at least, by my experiment: that if one advances confidently in the direction of his dreams, and endeavors to live the life in which he has imagined, he will meet with a success unexpected in common hours."

Henry David Thoreau

G. Keller

Chapter One

Any minute my phone alarm would light up and ring *Impossible Journey*, gently demanding me to rise. *Impossible journey.* I remember picking the ringtone when mom bought me the phone last year. My friends all had their favorite songs as ringtones, but that cost money and even the small amount of $1.99 made me feel guilty. I knew mom could barely afford the phone, so I carefully listened to all the free choices, several times, not liking any of them, really. Finally, I settled on *Impossible Journey.* It sounded smooth, quiet, sort of sad at first—slow and low, but then the notes lifted and picked up pace, leaving a bright, staccato, hopeful feeling at the end. I could start each day that way.

The truth is I am always awake when the *Impossible Journey* ringtone comes to life. Mom usually works the early morning shift at McCormick's Discount Department Store and purposely clanks around the kitchen, sending her passive aggressive message to all of us that she is the most responsible, dutiful, hardest working member of the household, and we – dad and me- are lazy creatures still sleeping at 6:15 am.

I usually pretend to be asleep, so I don't have to talk to her. The only conversation she knows how to have isn't really a conversation. It is more of a drill sergeant 'to do' list, given to me whenever our paths cross: *Vivian, unload the dishwasher and fold the clothes in the dryer; Vivian, your bathroom needs scrubbing. Be sure to use the bleach free tile scum product; Vivian, sweep the front porch and water the flowers in the courtyard.* I can't even think of the last time we actually had a conversation that didn't include an order.

As I lay waiting for her to exit the back door to the garage, I realized how quiet she had been this morning. I probably wouldn't have even woken up before *Impossible Journey* if my internal clock wasn't automatically programmed to wake me. She hadn't banged dishes loudly in the kitchen or stomped her high heels down the hallway like usual. She moved around the house with quiet care as if trying not to disturb us. This made me even more curious as to what she was doing, but not so much that I got up to check it out. I just preened my ears to listen to her stealthy movements. Had she gone into my bathroom? Odd. I thought I heard a slight creak of the door. Had she peeked into my room?

I thought I smelled a whiff of her signature scent, *Oscar de la Renta* perfume.

I finally rose after hearing the garage door close the second time and headed straight for the bathroom. There, taped to the mirror over the sink was a white envelope labeled: Vivian. A fleeting thought was that she had decided to write my chores down formally, but a pang in my gut said this was not a 'to do' list. The way she moved around this morning was different. I opened the letter, and a sudden chill trickled down my spine.

Dear Vivian,

This is the hardest decision I have ever made. I just can't do this anymore. Maybe if I'm gone your dad will finally restart his life. I have tried everything I know how to do, but it hasn't worked. This may seem drastic, but it is the only other thing I know to do.

Goodbye Viv, I love you.

Mom.

Chapter Two

Deep down, I knew it would come to this. We were all walking around pretending things would change after 'the incident', but nothing was changing. Well, one thing had changed. The first year, mom and dad fought viciously, spewing hateful names at each other. Mom would yell how stupid he was for making such a grave mistake. That he was probably drunk during the operation. That he had destroyed our family and our reputation. That now we wouldn't be able to finish our remodel. That we would lose the house. That she had to go back to work.

He would yell back what a materialistic bitch she was. Uncaring. That he drank because of the constant pressure she put on him to make money. That he didn't want this big house and expensive remodel.

The same yell fest was repackaged in several different styles but with the same theme over and over for a year. After those months of hateful performances, they slipped into a scarier fight. A silent fight. They didn't speak to one another anymore. Ever. Mom worked— often double shifts, came home, ate something, showered, and went to bed. When she saw me, she just gave me chores to do. Which I did dutifully. Anything to help relieve her workload, her sadness.

Dad never left the couch. Never. He must have to use the bathroom and eat or fill his wine glass, but I never saw it. The past two years had become an excruciatingly long stretched-out version of those moments before a bomb goes off. Tension building. No one speaking. Everyone waiting for the explosion.

Today was the day for change. A silent explosion showering invisible shrapnel in mother's wake.

Enduring the prickly pain, I walked back to my room and picked up my cell phone to call her. It went directly to voice mail. Mailbox full. I texted *Where are you?* I waited. Nothing.

I read the letter again. That was it? Six short sentences? Not an explanation of where she was going? When she would call me? If she would call me? Six sentences that sounded so final. Like I would never see her again. That can't be right. She wouldn't do that....

would she? Even though I never heard mom threaten to leave dad, I could see her divorcing him after everything that happened. She didn't have the love for him she once did. She lost all respect for him after the 'incident.' Divorce, yes, but to just disappear and leave a six-sentence note? This seemed surreal.

Over the last year, Mom had become distant and cold, but I attributed her withdrawal to our circumstances. I never doubted she loved me. I never thought she could leave me. And the way this short note was worded was weird. It didn't really sound like her. So abrupt. So mysterious. It didn't sound like she planned on having any contact with me or dad again. I just couldn't accept this. I didn't believe it. I was worth more than six sentences. I am her only daughter. She loves me. Maybe she didn't write much because she didn't know what she was going to do for sure. That had to be it. She just wasn't sure.

I called her again. Voicemail full. Again. Voicemail full. I spam texted her, 'Where are you?' over and over in a panic- induced frenzy. *Message unsent.* What the hell was going on?

I called McCormick's Department Store. The automatic messaging service spewed out a message saying they weren't open yet.

With the letter in my hand, I walked out to the living room to tell Dad. I stopped and stared at him. He was asleep on the couch, like always. Half-drunk glass of wine on the coffee table. His beard matted from lack of caring. I used to be able to tell what stage of depression he was in by the length of his beard. When bits of food were visibly stuck in it, he was usually rock bottom and on the verge of a temporary rebound. He would have a burst of hope and shower, shave, and get dressed. Like he was going on a job interview--maybe he was--or at least attempt a come-back after 'the incident.' Then the beard would begin to grow back, and his naps would turn into days and nights of constant slumber, a visible showcase of gradually giving up.

The beard had gotten so long and unruly that I couldn't even calculate the last hopeful shave. I didn't see any food bits, but I don't think he was eating much anymore. His body looked like a skeleton with skin, making his beard seem cartoonish against a stick-figure sketch. I suddenly wondered if he was slowly killing himself, and mom and I were letting it happen, like accomplices in a murder. Worry engulfed me. Tonight, I would microwave a can of chicken soup and make him eat it. I would do that every night to give him some strength. Strength enough to shave and shower. Strength enough to have a burst of hope.

I stood there looking around the house. Concrete floor where carpet and tile had once been. Exposed wood-framed walls with dangling electrical wires, enabling you to see from one room to the next. Gutted kitchen with only a refrigerator plugged into a hanging outlet and a usable sink encased in the old kitchen cabinetry. A flimsy folding table shoved against the wall with a coffee maker, microwave, toaster, and crockpot. A camper's kitchen. A kitchen so the opposite of the elaborate, modern kitchen mom had envisioned that I'm surprised she stayed this long.

An opened box of framed photos caked with dust sat on top of a stack of decorating and remodeling magazines, another reminder of how long we had been living in a construction zone. I could hardly see the picture sitting on top. It was mom's favorite-- Mom, Dad, and me at the Museum of Art's Mary Cassatt collection tour. I wiped the glass a little so I could see us better. A better us. A happier us. I lingered my stare at mom in the picture. She was stunning. Everywhere we went, people stopped to stare at her. In this picture, she looked like a movie star—prettier really. Her hair was the perfect honey blonde with highlights that screamed expensive. Her cornflower blue eyes and polished white teeth made people wonder if she was famous. I shifted my eyes to the picture of Dad, handsome in a suit, smiling proudly with a gleam that said, 'look who I landed and the lovely daughter we produced.'

I set the picture back down on top of the other dusty pictures and magazines. Magazines that drew up images of how excited mom had been, pining over and over the photos inside, dog earing pages of her favorite styles, excitedly cutting out her top pics and creating a three-ring binder of her dream house. The white binder labeled 'Fantasy Home' lay next to the pile and was not only dusty but turning a faint yellow from sitting stagnant for so long.

Everything had come to a screeching halt the day of 'the incident'--dad had operated on the wrong eye of a patient, making the patient blind. Dad was sued, lost his medical license, and life changed overnight.

Mom and dad put all their money into purchasing this mansion in the most prestigious neighborhood on the north side of town—the 'new money' side of town. New money, as mom explained to me when we purchased the house, was the area of town that was growing with people who made their money themselves and didn't inherit it from their family. The 'old money' side of town was on the far south side of Portofino, where mansions were one- of- a-kind worldly estates gracing the shores of the Gulf of Mexico or the banks of Putter's Bay with million-dollar yachts parked in the back for easy Gulf access.

Mom would drive by these American castles with impressed awe and say, 'Maybe one day…'

That one day would never happen because they had taken out a line of credit for the remodel and as soon as dad lost his license, the bank froze the credit. No more remodel. We were stuck.

Mom went to work as a clerk at McCormick's—humiliating to her as she constantly told us the first year. Her paycheck barely kept us going—another fact she constantly reminded us of. I couldn't believe she chose to work at McCormick's. She had always made fun of people who shopped there, like the store was cheap and the clientele was 'less than'. I asked her why she got a job there and not Neiman Marcus or Saks Fifth Avenue or one of the boutiques on Third Street South where the clothes were her style, classy and chic and too expensive for ordinary people. She simply replied that she wasn't going to wait on her 'friends'. What she didn't add was 'former' because ever since 'the incident', mom hadn't socialized with the high society 'new money' circle of snobs she once did.

I turned around and decided I would wait until after school to show dad the letter, after I fed him some chicken soup. Shaking off everything that was happening, I shifted into auto mode. Get ready for school. Deal with this later. I shoved mom's letter in my bathroom drawer, got ready for school, grabbed my backpack, and walked out the front door to catch the bus. I passed Winston at the guard gate and waved hello with a smile, concealing anything abnormal happening in my life. He smiled and nodded his usual good morning gesture. The bus passed my house as it pulled away from the curb, and I stared at the regal facade. It was impossible to believe that such a beautiful, luxurious home was an empty shell inside.

Chapter Three

I moved through my day at school with fake functional formality. Easy to do in middle school where everybody is a phony. I was just one of hundreds alluding normalcy. Brianna, Bella, and Sarah didn't notice anything out of the ordinary about me. At lunch, they just gossiped about the 'losers' in various classes and laughed at 'stupid' things they had done. I barely listened, but laughed at the appropriate times, appearing to be one of the gang as usual.

After lunch, I slipped into the bathroom and locked myself in a stall. I texted mom again. Message unsent. I called McCormick's. I pressed zero for customer service. Someone answered.

I said, "Is Victoria James there?"

"Victoria? She quit." The woman sounded rushed.

"Do you know where she went?" I asked.

"No, honey. No one does. She just quit without notice. Disappeared. Who is calling?"

In slow motion, I clicked off the phone and stood frozen in the stall, unable to move, unable to swallow, unable to breathe.

Quit. Disappeared. Where did she go?

***

On the bus ride home, I went over in my head countless ways to tell dad mom was gone. I imagined how he would react. I practiced my reactions to these scenarios. I definitely had to feed him first. He would never eat if I told him about the letter. He needed food to function. My most hopeful delusion was that he would eat the soup, thanking me, telling me he was sorry. I would tell him about the letter, and he would grab my shoulders, look me in the eye with determination, and say, 'I have a plan. I am going to go out and get a job. I don't care what I do, but it will be something to make you and your mom proud of me. I will get her back. Everything will be fine. We will finish this house and sell it, and find a nice, smaller one. Everything will be even better than before.'

But all that imaginary mind practice was a waste.

When I got off the bus, walked up the driveway, and opened the garage door with my clicker, Dad's car was gone, and Mom's car had not returned. Two vacant spots with boxes stacked neatly along the perimeter and piled to the ceiling. Boxes filled with brand new cabinets, sinks, plumbing fixtures, lighting fixtures, flooring, and tools, waiting to transform the hollow interior.

Why was dad's car gone?

I hurried down the concrete hallway to the sparse living room/dad's bedroom. Dad wasn't on the couch ready for my prepared presentation. Had he decided to shave, shower and come back to life momentarily? Without my soup? Without my news? Maybe mom had left him a letter, too. Maybe the letter prompted him to get up and fix everything. Fix us.

I walked back down the concrete hallway.

Silence.

I slipped passed the laundry room and into my parents' bedroom – or mom's bedroom the last three years since dad took to the couch.

Empty.

I hurried back to my wing of the house. Set my backpack in my room and glanced at my bathroom door. I needed to see that letter again. Maybe I missed something.   I opened the door quickly and stopped abruptly.

Laying on the counter was another envelope. What was going on? I pulled open the drawer where I thought I shoved Mom's letter, briefly thinking that maybe I left it on the counter by accident, but there it was, crumpled next to a tube of hair gel.

I grabbed the new envelope and frantically opened it.

Dear Viv,

I feel like such a huge failure, and I can no longer face you or your mom. I want you to know how much I love you both and that is why I am leaving. Your mom can find someone new who can take better care of her and you. I wish I could be better. I have tried. Please know that. I am sorry. I cannot watch you and your mom suffer any more. This is all my fault. Please forgive me.

Love,

Dad

Chapter Four

I was alone.

I texted dad first. *Where are you?*

Then mom. *Where are you?*

Fear snaked its way through my body. Not an 'I'm afraid of the boogieman' kind of fear. I had lived in this neighborhood for nearly three years and always felt safe. Winston, the day guard, and a rotating group of night guards were only a few steps from my front door. And it was virtually impossible to get into this neighborhood. Well, I suppose it was possible, but it would be hard. The tall stone wall protected the wealthy residents like a modern fortress and if that wasn't enough, several TV monitors flanked the inside of the guard house giving Winston and his posse boring, one-star programming to constantly view because nothing ever happened here. Most of the residents barely spent three months living in Royal Palm Estates, January-February-March, when temperatures dipped uncomfortably cold in their own hometowns up north.

No, this fear was a 'how am I going to survive' kind of fear. Did I stay here alone and not tell anyone? Did I say something to Winston? No, he would call the police, and I might have to go to a foster home or something. Out of the question. Foster homes weren't for kids like me. Foster kids had parents who beat them, did drugs, prostitution, were drunk or in jail. Not kids like me. My dad was a doctor. My mom was a doctor's wife. We lived in a Country Club Community with a brick wall and a guard to keep those people out.

But with that thought, my chest tightened. I tried to swallow, but my throat fought me as I forced down a gulp. Reality hit me like a punch in the face. My mom *was* a doctor's wife. My dad *was* a doctor. My mom *is* a person who left me with a dad who *is* a drunk and now has disappeared. How was my situation any different from a kid in foster care? It wasn't. Face it, Vivian. It wasn't.

Should I tell Brianna, Sarah, or Bella? No. I couldn't. But they are your best friends. My mind flashed to third grade when Byron Finster announced to Mrs. Robinson, our teacher, that he was late for school because all his furniture was in his front yard when he got home the day before, and he had to take a city bus from the homeless shelter to get to school that day. Brianna snickered and whispered to me, '*Take a look at his backpack.*' My eyes darted reluctantly to a dirty backpack with a large hole in the bottom corner exposing an unraveling spiral notebook. Glancing back at Brianna, her face smug with disgust, I just looked away pretending to be distracted by Mrs. Robinson's gentle reaction to Byron's confessional. She redirected the class to our morning routine and pulled Byron aside to whisper something that appeared sweet and thoughtful. No, I wasn't going to tell Brianna or Bella or Sarah anything.

What about Langston? Could you tell him? Never. But he is your boyfriend, Vivian. He told you he loved you. Something in my gut told me his love had contingencies. No, it was best not to tell my friends, or my boyfriend, anything yet.

I had become a master at separating my school life from my home life, like I was two completely different people. I wasn't ready to become one just yet. Besides, I bet mom or dad or both would realize their mistake and come home apologizing. Probably soon. One of them had to. Where would they go anyway? A hotel? They didn't have the money for that. A friend's house? What friends? My parents hadn't gone or done anything with anyone since the incident.

One of them had to return soon. I would just stay here, alone, until that happened.

I took a deep breath and sighed a relief sigh, relaxing the panic that so recently consumed me, and walked to my bathroom to turn on the water and wash the worry off my face.

The spigot sputtered and spat violently for a quick second, like a cat coughing up a hairball of water. Then stopped. Nothing. Not even a drop.

I ran to mom's bathroom to try her sink. Not even a sputter or a spat. Just the echo of an empty pipe. Kitchen sink. Nothing.

I was out of water.

Chapter Five

3:33pm brightly stared at me in crisp clean white numbers. I checked my texts. Nothing. I clicked off the screen, laid the phone on my bed and fell back staring at the ceiling.

Mom stopped paying the water bill.

I wonder if that is why she left. She couldn't pay the bills anymore and left before the water ran out. Coward. It was Ok for us not to have water, but her? She would rather leave than deal with this tragedy.

But where? Was she secretly seeing someone else? Cheating on dad? There were days when she left early and didn't come home until late. She said she was working double shifts. Maybe she was leading a double life. It was possible. I was leading a double life—school me and home me. Was there a work mom and a home mom? Definitely possible.

Or she was planning her escape from this dead man walking existence and instead of paying the bills, she was hoarding the money, so she had enough to survive on her own. Selfish.

She knew dad hadn't worked in almost three years, and he hadn't given us reason to think he would start any time soon. So basically, her having enough money to start over was more important than us having water. Hate found every cavity of my brain.

What modern day luxury was next? Electricity? My phone? Mom always complained about the homeowner's dues each month that paid for the guard gate, yard guys, and clubhouse membership. I'm sure she stopped paying those, too. Would the grass grow so long, gradually giving the outside world a glimpse of the truth? How long could I really hide here alone if they didn't return soon?

Make a plan, I told myself. *It will stop the panic.* This is one thing my mother taught me. When I was in the fifth grade, I had a big project on the history of Florida that I procrastinated starting until a week before it was due. I had all quarter to complete it, and I just kept putting it off because the due date seemed so far away. When I realized the magnitude of what I needed to do in only one week, I had a total meltdown, crying so uncontrollably that mom shook me to listen to her. She said, "Vivian, make a plan. Just map out your week and plan each thing you must do. It will help. I promise." She was right. It helped. I worked harder than I had my whole elementary school existence, but planning worked. I got the project done. I have used the 'make a plan' technique several times during middle school, and it works.

I wonder if mom made a plan for her escape. Probably.

I sat up and opened my bedside table, pulling out a small gold jewelry box where I kept my money. Babysitting money. I laid it out and began to count. $187.53. This total would have been more, but like an idiot, I bought clothes and make-up and stupid, unnecessary stuff. $187.53 was all I had left. Not even close to pay bills, but it would be enough for groceries until one of my pathetic parents faced their problems and returned. The grocery store was less than a mile down the street. I could take my backpack and walk there or ride my bike and get some peanut butter and bread. I could last a long time on $187.53 if I just ate that.

What about water? I needed water to drink, shower and wash my hair. Oh no, the toilet. Does the toilet work without water? I ran back to the bathroom and tried flushing the toilet. Nothing. How would I go to the bathroom? The house would start smelling like one of those disgusting portable toilets. And I couldn't keep up my two separate lives if I started showing up at school with greasy hair and smelly armpits.

Suddenly, I remembered the clubhouse. There were showers and lockers in the clubhouse by the community pool and restaurant. I hadn't been there in a long time, but I could take up swimming and just shower and blow dry my hair there when I got home from school. I could use the toilet there, too.

Water problem solved for now. Sort of. I wasn't sure what to do if I had a bathroom emergency. I couldn't exactly run to the clubhouse every time I needed to pee. I will think about that later.

I plugged in my phone to get charged. So far, the phone still worked and there was still electricity.

I had to get over to the pool before it got too late. I changed into a swimsuit and pulled over shorts and a t-shirt. I emptied homework and books out of my backpack and tossed in underwear, a bra, some shampoo, a towel, and an empty jug to store water for the night. I slipped into flip flops, unplugged my phone, and headed out the door towards the clubhouse. Just a country club rich kid going for a swim. Becoming my second personality was as easy as changing into a swimsuit.

I passed the guardhouse casually, looking at my phone for any texts like a normal teenager. Winston was standing outside the sliding door reviewing a clipboard.

He looked up and nodded, "Going for a swim, Vivian?"

I loved his island accent. "Yep."

"Have a good time."

Bing.

Text message: Verizon bill overdue. Click here to pay.

I quickly sent mom another text. *Where are you? You need to pay the phone bill. And come home!!! There is no water! Help. Please.*

Auto text response: *text message unsent.*

Don't panic, Vivian. Remember, you made a plan.

Chapter Six

Country Club Girl. That is what they call me at school. I liked it. It made me feel important. It reminded me of the way things were before 'the incident.' It helped me keep my worlds separate. As long as people called me Country Club Girl, I was full of hope. Hope that things would get back to normal. As if saying Country Club Girl over and over enough would will the bills to get paid. Dad to get a job. The remodel to magically get done so mom could be happy. So we all could be happy.

I got the nickname the summer between fifth and sixth grade. We had just moved into Royal Palm Estates my fifth-grade year. Mom told me to plan a pool party as my first attempt at becoming a future up and coming socialite. I remember her saying that and giggling.

I invited Brianna, Bella and Sarah, Sterling, Langston, and Grady. We ordered lunch at the clubhouse and ate gourmet hamburgers and thick cut fries with ketchup in silver cups instead of out of the plastic bottle. We drank fresh squeezed lemonade with lemon slices floating on the top, telling the world that this lemonade was better than regular out-of-the can powdered lemonade.

Brianna had taken a sip, closed her eyes, and said, "I could get used to this country club life." She opened her eyes, laughed, and called me lucky Country Club Girl. Then we all jumped into the pool, and everyone started calling me Country Club Girl. Langston kept chasing me and grabbing me under the water, pretending to be some sea creature attacking me. He splashed me, laughing, calling me Country Club Girl in a way that suggested he liked it, too. He liked me—country club me.

We joked all that afternoon about how we were going to rule middle school. Country Club Girl and her court. Like the lavish King Henry VIII's inner circle of beautiful, wealthy maidens and gentlemen, living the noble, superior life.

And we did. When sixth grade finally started, Langston and I were a 'thing' and everyone at school wanted to be our friend.

Then the incident happened. At home, everything went spiraling out of control. But I discovered something immediately after my home life began unraveling. Middle schoolers didn't notice. Everyone at school was wrapped up in their own self-centered worlds, acting as if the daily dramas were all that existed in their lives. And that was perfectly fine by me. Actually, better than fine. Country Club Girl by day helped me survive the nights.

Now, surviving the nights was taking on a whole new dimension. I had figured out my temporary fix for not having water, but what about my phone? How was I going to survive without a phone?

I still couldn't accept that mom or dad wouldn't be home soon. One of them had to feel guilty, turn around and come back. What were the odds that both of my parents would choose the exact same day to give up and run away? A million to one? Had they been together so long that even though they hardly ever spoke to each other anymore, their minds still thought alike?

I had the sudden urge to go back to the house to see if one of them was home.

I got out of the pool and quickly ran into the locker room to shower and change. I was relieved no one was here. It was after 4:00 and you wouldn't think anyone belonged to this club. Mom had told me once that old people did all their activity in the morning. By this time, they were heading to the early bird dinner special.

Since it was already April, most of them had gone back up north. I was glad. I didn't need some nosy neighbor asking me questions.

I toweled off and got dressed. I felt fresh and awake. I filled my jug with water from the water fountain just outside the locker room because it was the coldest. I put it in my backpack along with my wet bathing suit and towel and zipped it closed. A teenager walking with a big plastic jug of water might look weird. Winston might wonder what was going on. I had to look normal. I had to look like Country Club Girl.

Chapter Seven

I hustled up the driveway and unzipped the small side zipper on my backpack to grab the garage remote. I quickly clicked the button, desperately hoping for at least one car in the garage. The garage door didn't open. Maybe I didn't click hard enough. I clicked again. Nothing. I frantically clicked over and over again like an impatient infant. Why wasn't the garage door opening? This was my only way into the house. I never used a key. I didn't even know where a key to the house was. I always used the garage opener. We left the door from the garage into the house open, so once you were in the garage, you could get in.

Oh no. Suddenly, I realized something, and an alarm went off in me so quickly, panic prevented swallowing. The garage door needed electricity. Another unpaid bill. My mind immediately went to that day. That day when I discovered how bad things had gotten. Mom and I had come home from the grocery store, and the garage door wouldn't open. Mom told me to stay in the car. She grabbed the few bags of food we had purchased and went to the front door of the house. She emerged in what seemed like forever with dad's bike. She popped the trunk of her SUV and slid it in the back and slammed the door shut. I was confused. I asked her what was going on and she replied, "Don't worry. Things will get better." Still confused but not wanting to probe any further for fear of mom saying things that would freak me out, I sat in silence. You couldn't even hear breathing as mom drove to a part of town I had never been before. I remember looking at her face and seeing the contorted worry meshed with anger carved all over her features. She kept looking at the gas gauge and back to the road. My eyes followed hers to the gas gauge, and I noticed the bright orange light and the needle lying flat on the bottom marker. Her body was rigid and leaning forward as if that posture would somehow get the car to where we were going before running out of gas. Then the truck sighed a few heavy sighs, and mom managed to maneuver the massive vehicle to the right side of the road at an entrance to a neighborhood.

Before she could say or do anything, a police officer pulled up behind us and turned on his lights. Mom quickly got out, and I heard her start to lie.

"Officer, my daughter wants a new phone, you know these kids. So, I'm trying to teach her the value of money, and I'm making her sell her bike at the pawn shop a few blocks away. But I didn't realize I was out of gas. I just need to get to that shop, and then I'll go get gas."

I watched her through the rear-view mirror, running her hands through her thick blonde hair and flashing her movie star smile. Gone was the contorted anger from moments ago. I could tell the cop was enamored with her. Men's voices changed whenever they got the privilege of talking to my mom, my beautiful mom. They sounded like puppy dogs begging for a bone, almost whimpering at the attention she gives them.

This cop was no different. "I'll give you girls a lift." And just like that. Dad's bike was in the trunk of the police car, and mom and I were being escorted to a place called The Priceless Pawn.

Dad had a super expensive bike, but the pawn guy only gave mom $450 for it. I was so embarrassed about what was going on that I was in shock and said nothing. The policeman drove us to a gas station and mom filled a red plastic jug that the officer had in his trunk with gas. He returned us to our car and offered to fill what little gas the red jug held into our SUV. Mom thanked him profusely. We then drove to a building where mom paid the electricity bill. We had a little left over, so she drove to another gas station to put more gas in the car.

That is when I knew we were in deep trouble. Mom had been convincing me that dad would work through his depression, and everything would be OK, but this incident proved her wrong. We were not OK. We were far from OK. We were hawking stuff at a pawn shop in a seedy part of town kind of not OK.

Now I realized that Mom had stopped paying everything, leaving before having to face the consequences of her actions. Leaving before another pawn shop incident.

No water.

No phone.

No electricity.

How was I going to get into the house? Trying to appear calm, I walked up the front steps in the unlikely event the front door was open. I pressed the handle. Locked tight. I walked around back to the pool cage enclosure's side screen door. Sometimes it was open. I clicked the door handle. Open. *Whew.* At least I was in the patio, somewhat away from the view of neighbors.

There were three sliding doors. One to a guest bedroom, one to the living room, and one to the kitchen.

Locked…. Locked…. Locked….

I flopped on an old moldy lounge chair. I stared at the empty, cavernous pool, also waiting a renovation. Had mom been planning her departure from us for over a month? Secretly stashing extra cash for her getaway? Or had she given up like dad? Too hapless to find the strength to pay a bill. Then skipping town when she came to her senses and realized what she had done but didn't have the money to fix the problem. And what about dad? He hadn't paid a bill in almost three years. Or gone to a store for groceries. Or cleaned. Or worked. He barely got off the couch. How would he know if a bill was due or not? He wouldn't. His escape on the same day as mom was merely a coincidence. And an odd coincidence. After years of immobility, where would he suddenly go?

Think, Vivian. Think.

The sun was dropping fast now and beating down on me like a theater stage spotlight. I was a one-woman act who had forgotten my lines and was now searching the audience for a clue to help me continue and not embarrass myself anymore.

I left my backpack on the patio floor and decided to walk around the house and check every window. I had

41

to do this quickly, so I wouldn't draw suspicion if a neighbor saw me trying to break into my house. I doubted that would happen because the neighborhood felt abandoned, like Winston and I were the only two people in the whole development. I hadn't heard a car or seen a person walk by since I got off the bus.

After the third window, I was losing any hope of getting into my house. I *had* to get in. I just *had* to. The last possible chance was the French door off my parents' bedroom. There was a concrete walled courtyard with a rod-iron gate-like door surrounding a pretty patio. Before 'the incident,' mom had almost completed the renovation of my bedroom and my parents' bedroom, so we could live more comfortably while the rest of the house went into demolition mode.

One of the changes she made was a beautiful single paned French door to replace the ugly sliding window. Mom insisted that she was going to have one place in the house she could go to that was nice during the construction.

The iron gate was locked. I looked over both shoulders and didn't see anyone, so I lodged one foot on one of the horizontal iron crossbars, hoisted myself up to find a spot for my other foot, swung my leg over the top of the gate and jumped down. My heart was pulsing and pumping. Please be open. Please.

I pushed down on the lever-like handle. Locked. I looked closely through the crack between the double-paned doors to see if it was dead-bolted. It wasn't. I fiercely began to jiggle the handle up and down, up and down, up and down, more violently each time. I could feel the lock loosening just a little. I pulled up so forcefully, the handle suddenly broke off, and I tumbled back, falling to the ground.

Crap. Now what? I buried my head in my hands, still clutching the broken off handle.

What was I going to do? I didn't know what time it was, but I guessed around 5:30. Mom or dad still had plenty of time to come to their senses and come home. I decided to return to the back patio and rest on the old lounge chair and just hope one of them comes home.

Chapter Eight

I must have fallen asleep because when I opened my eyes, it was pitch black. A faint orange glow shone from the closest streetlight. Streetlights were practically nonexistent in Royal Palm Estates and gave off just enough light to get you home, but not enough light to really see. My dad had commented once that these rich snowbirds didn't want a bright light to keep them from their precious sleep. I remember him saying that not because the barely-there streetlight was so interesting, but because dad's tone made me feel like he set himself apart from these 'rich people' even though at the time that is what we were, too. Not snowbirds, but rich enough to buy a home here and gut it out to completely renovate it. It was the first time I thought mom and dad weren't on the same page with this whole house purchase and remodel.

I had no idea now what time it was. The stillness of the night made me realize my worst fear. No one had come home. I was really all alone. Now I was going to have to break into the house somehow without making any noise. A broken window in the middle of the night would stir attention, no doubt. There had to be someone living here in April, and we were so close to the gate entrance, a night guard would surely hear me if I smashed glass.

Suddenly, I had an idea. I searched through my backpack and there at the bottom of the side pouch was exactly what I was looking for—bobby pins. I often put my long hair in a loose bun on top of my head during the day at school and then let it down on the bus ride home, shoving the bobby pins into my backpack. I gently slipped out the screen door, quietly closing the door behind me. Like a cat burglar, I slunk around the house to the courtyard off my mom's room again. I shoved the bobby pin in my hair and scaled the iron gate, easier this time, and saw the broken handle I had left lying on the ground.

I pulled the pin out of my hair and bent it flat, so it was twice as long. There was a tiny hole in the center of where the handle had broken off. I had remembered this trick from a time I spent the night at Brianna's house, and we accidentally locked ourselves out of her bedroom.

She did this trick to open the door. Hopefully, it would work. I stuck the pin in the hole and poked over and over several times. Nothing. Exhausted, I sat down and leaned back against the French door, when it gently opened, and I fell back into mom's bedroom.

Chapter Nine

I wish I had a pet right now. A dog or a cat. No particular preference really. Just a furry creature to pet and calm me down. I never knew such blackness. The faint orange from the distant streetlight that barely glowed on the patio was nonexistent in the house. This kind of darkness was scarier than I ever imagined anything could be. I noticed my chest heaving up and down as I lay on my back on top of the covers. The air was getting sticky. It was April and already hot. Mom told me once that the only reason people started moving to south Florida was the invention of air conditioning. Otherwise, she said, no one would ever live in this hot, humid, mold factory.

If I had a dog right now, she would lick my face and make me relax and possibly cool me down. Mom hated animals. She always claimed she liked them, but whenever I begged for one, she had some excuse. When I was little, before we moved, her excuse was that I wasn't old enough to care for an animal. Then when we moved and started the remodel, she said a construction zone was no place to train a dog and a cat would be scared of the noise. I pretty much realized that she didn't really want a pet. I figured if we ever did finish the remodel, her next excuse would have been that the house was so nice, a pet would smell it up.

A purr from a cat or a lick from a dog was what I needed right now. Then again, in my current dilemma, a pet would be another mouth to feed. But I wouldn't care. I would eat less. I would rather hold something than eat something.

After falling into mom's room, I grabbed the broken handle and bolted the door. I fumbled to my bedroom and crawled into bed. I had no idea what time it was. I had no idea if my parents were ever coming back. I had no idea if I would go to school tomorrow.

Oh God, school.

I have had perfect attendance my entire middle school career. This was a big deal at Beachside Middle School. It was April, and I am an eighth grader, and I have never missed a day. Every morning, Mr. Kingsly, the assistant principal, would greet me with a big hello as I walked across the courtyard on my way to homeroom and remind me how I was going be the first Beachside student in three years who was going to get perfect attendance for *all* of middle school.

I *really* wanted to stay home tomorrow. I wanted to be here when one of my parents came to their senses and returned. I wanted to yell at them and say, 'How could you do this to me?' I wanted to hug them and say, 'Everything would be OK.' Besides, I never blew my hair dry at the clubhouse after my shower. I was going to do that here, at home. But with no electricity and getting locked out, I hadn't even thought about it. My hair was flat and gross. Brianna, Bella, Sarah and especially Langston would know something was up. Besides being 'Country Club Girl', my long hair was one of Langston's favorite things about me. But then, if I didn't go to school, Mr. Kingsly, Brianna and the gang, and my teachers would all wonder what was up because they knew how badly I wanted the perfect attendance award. Not going to school would alert someone to my situation, and I didn't want that.

I decided to get up at the first hint of light and go back to the clubhouse and shower again and blow dry my hair. I didn't want anything to appear out of the ordinary. Mom or Dad had to be lying in bed right now, somewhere, thinking about what an awful thing they had done, and return tomorrow.

Where had they gone? I wondered. My grandparents had all passed away and both of my parents were only children. If mom had been putting on a double life, like me, I seriously doubt she would confess to a friend what was going on. In fact, she had pretty much cut off contact with any friends after the incident. I never heard her on the phone with anyone. I never saw her go out with anyone. She just worked and came home to sleep, doing double shifts when she could. Then, up the next day to do it all over again.

Mom must have been saving some money, especially since the bills had gone unpaid. She could last a while in a cheap motel. Mom in a cheap motel. That was a hard picture to form in my head.

Dad, on the other hand, was a complete mystery. Dad had barely gotten up from the couch in almost three years except to get wine, so leaving the house at all was a miracle. Could he possibly go completely off the grid? Become one of those homeless people living under a bridge, rummaging through garbage? I think he could. He would grow his beard so long roaches and spiders would crawl in it. I could see him curled up in a ball next to a scraggly scrub bush. It was a pathetic image, but not that much worse than how he had been living here. He would just be doing it outside without the condescending eyes of Mom and the pleading eyes of me. Yes, I could now imagine him not coming home, ever.

And Mom? I could now imagine her not coming home, too, searching for what she wasn't getting here or escaping what she was getting here. Either way, I could now picture both of my parents gone. For good.

I had to go to school. I had no choice. They might be gone forever. I couldn't stay home from school forever. Someone would come get me. *That,* can't happen. Besides, the perfect attendance award came with a $100 gift card to Target and if no one comes home to rescue me, Country Club Girl will need the money.

Chapter Ten

The next morning was Tuesday, and I decided to go to school, but I couldn't sleep. I just laid on my bed, listening for a sound of any kind, but none came. Complete blackness and complete silence. It made me think of that song my dad loved, *The Sound of Silence*. Before 'the incident,' he used to sing it in the car, clean shaven, with his deep, baritone voice. *Hello darkness my old friend. I've come to talk to you again.* His eyes would twinkle a smile while the sad words bellowed and filled the entire cavity of the car. I remember thinking of the dichotomy between his countenance and the context of the lyrics.

I sang that line softly, breaking the stillness, but I never got past those two lines. I couldn't remember the rest of the words. Just as well. My voice sounded shrill, weak, crackly, and pathetic, and instead of the words filling the black space of my room, they seemed to disintegrate immediately when they emerged from my lips and hit the air. As if the air was a fire extinguisher squelching the life out of each syllable.

It wasn't just the darkness and silence that kept me awake. My mind was full of survival plans. What would I eat? How long could I last with the money I had? How would I use the bathroom in an emergency? How to use the clubhouse locker room without drawing suspicion? How long could I last without telling someone what was going on? What would happen if someone discovered me here alone? How to get in and out of the house without getting locked out and yet keeping the house secure? My mind was racing with plausible answers.

At the first hint of light, I found some duct tape and secured the latch down so the broken French door in mom's room swung open. Mrs. Kamen had done this last year when teachers were told they had to keep their doors locked at all times. She occasionally forgot her keys and would do this trick to get in and out of her classroom. Now I could get in and out of this door and keep the front door locked. I didn't want anyone snooping around when I was at school, and the French door was at least surrounded by a locked courtyard.

Then I got everything I needed for school and put it in my backpack. I passed Winston on my way to the clubhouse, and he nodded hello and said, "Another swim?" I smiled back acting chipper. "Yep." I realized a second swim in the last twenty-four hours might look odd to him, so I quickly added, "I am going to try out for the high school swim team. I am in training mode." He smiled, said good-luck and went back to his guardhouse.

I swam a couple of laps and the cool pool felt like heaven. Refreshed and ready to switch into my second life, I showered, shampooed (using the clubhouse shampoo and conditioner to start saving money) and got dressed. I used the clubhouse hair dryer to style my hair so that no one could tell anything was out of the ordinary. I wrung out my swimsuit and found an empty locker that wasn't locked to hide it in for now. I doubted anyone would take it, but if they did, I had several others.

There was a clock in the locker room, and it said 7:45. The bus would be here in about 15 minutes.

I had forgotten to pack a lunch, but I wasn't hungry. I would just skip lunch today.

It was amazing how easy it was to lead a double life in middle school. And this week was especially easy because it was state testing week. The daily schedule was completely different, so lunches were all messed up. I didn't have to face Brianna, Bella, and Sarah or Langston and his friends. We were all going to shorter, different lunch times. People just ate and ran to their next class.

The rest of the week fell into a pattern, and I realized no one at school could tell that I was living alone. When I got on and off the bus, Winston didn't seem to act any differently towards me either.

At home, I rummaged through the garage and found the hurricane survival kit my parents put together the first year we were in the house. There had been a category four hurricane threatening to come our way and everybody freaked out. It went north of us, but we were completely prepared. The kit had a flashlight, batteries, and a portable radio/cd player, along with a first aid kit. I took all those things to my room. Now, I had light and a radio that I gave up on when I couldn't get a station that wasn't garbled with static, even with the antennae stretched out.

I meandered to the kitchen for something to eat. I kept the fridge closed to help it stay as cold as possible for as long as possible, and I ate the few items that were left in there immediately after the power went out. Yogurt, cheese, and milk for cereal. I skipped lunch again today and was ravenous. All I had left were two slices of bread and barely enough peanut butter to make a measly sandwich. I will have to go to the grocery store tomorrow. I inhaled the sandwich and walked back to my room.

Mentally and physically exhausted, I collapsed on my bed. I must have fallen asleep because when I woke, the room was pitch black. Tired of the dark, I flicked on the flashlight and followed the angles where the ceiling and wall met, slowly outlining the room. *'Hello darkness, my old friend. I've come to talk to you again.'* This time my voice didn't sound as shrill. Too exhausted to be frightened, my chest fell into a rhythmic movement, up and down, breathing deeply in and out. I wracked my brain for the next lines to that song. The heavy breathing must have helped clear my brain because suddenly I continued with *'because a vision softly creeping, left its seeds while I was sleeping, and the vision that was planted in my brain, still remains, within the sound of silence.'*

Suddenly, I saw a bug, in the corner, startled by the roaming flashlight, frozen still.

'Hello darkness, my new friend.'

Chapter Eleven

My mind was trying to wake me up, but my body was battling resistance. *'Get up! You need to get up and use the bathroom.'* Fiercely trying to comply with the request, my arms and legs rejected the plea and remained nailed to the bed. My head refused to lift off the pillow, feeling heavy like lead. The voice telling me to get up NOW seemed muffled, distant, and distorted. Suddenly, a warm liquid began leaking, wetting my underwear, forcing my body to finally answer the pleading request with a jolt out of bed. I clenched to stop the deluge and hurled myself to the garage, grabbed the first bucket I saw, squatted, and relieved myself into the plastic container.

After a sigh of sudden comfort, I removed the wet underwear, wrapped it in a plastic bag, and changed into my swimsuit. I checked to make sure I hadn't soiled the sheets. Luckily, I jumped up before any damage was done. Before slipping out the back courtyard to go wash off the urine smell, I dumped the yellow liquid at the base of a hedge and set the bucket down to pick up on my return. I don't know why I hadn't thought of a bucket before. It was an easy solution to my bathroom needs.

I was going to take and wash my underwear at the clubhouse but decided to just throw them away. I had plenty of underwear and couldn't risk some old lady, up for an early swim, catching me doing laundry in the locker room sink. No, best to just dump the evidence.

After rinsing off in the shower, I jumped in the pool. My swim was quick, and the shower was quicker. I wanted to get to the store before too many people arrived.

Once back home, I found a cup of coins in Mom's bathroom, and I added it to my money. I now had $198.04. My mind constantly waffled between thoughts of my parents never returning to hopes of my parents coming home. Whatever outcome was destined to happen, I had to see how far I could stretch this money. If I didn't spend more than $25 a week on groceries, I could last almost eight weeks. I *had* to hear from one of them in the next eight weeks.

I never did the grocery shopping, so I wasn't completely sure how much things cost, but I was about to find out. I put $25 dollars in my backpack and hid the remaining $173.04 in the jewelry box in the drawer of the table beside my bed. I didn't want to take any more than this so I wouldn't be tempted to overspend.

Wheeling Mom's bike from the garage, I had to bring it through the house since the garage door wouldn't open. I decided to take her bike because it had a basket on it to hold items. I leaned it against the wall outside the front door and hung my helmet on the handlebars, went back in to lock the front door, and then slipped out the duct taped French door off Mom's room. I swiftly climbed the locked iron gate and walked around to the front door to get my bike. This seemed a little elaborate, but I felt better keeping the front door locked.

***

Traffic wasn't bad because it was early on a Saturday. I didn't want to bump into anyone, so I figured I would get there as soon as it opened. I buckled my helmet and peddled past the guard house as if I was going to meet up with friends.

When I got to the grocery store, I realized I didn't really know where to put my bike. I decided to go up to the front door and lean it against the wall right next to the exit. I unclipped my helmet and shoved it in the bike basket.

Grabbing a cart, I slowly began walking up and down the aisles, looking at prices for the first time in my life. I couldn't buy anything that needed to be refrigerated, so I decided to walk over to the deli with precooked food items. The chicken tenders said $6.99 for 3 tenders. That was almost 1/3 of my money. I walked away from the deli and over to the produce section. Apples didn't need refrigeration, so I found the cheapest bag for $4.99. There were 12 apples so I figured I could make that stretch. Bananas were 61 cents a pound, so I weighed a bundle, and it came to three pounds. I added the bananas to the cart. There was a display of peanut butter with a sign 'BUY ONE GET ONE FREE'. I was already sick of peanut butter, but this would last me a long time, so I put two tubs of extra crunchy peanut butter in my cart for $4.98. My total was about $12 dollars.

This didn't give me much food, and I needed toilet paper (in case I had an emergency and had to use the bucket), toothpaste, deodorant, and pads for my period – which was due this week. The cheapest toilet paper was a four pack for $4.99. The smallest tube of toothpaste was $2.46. Cheapest deodorant $2.98. Cheapest pads $6.95. I was over my 25$.

I decided to put back the pads for my period and just go to the nurse this week and ask for a few. I'll tell her it is really bad, and hopefully she will give me several. I passed another 'BUY ONE GET ONE FREE' display of Ritz crackers for $3.50. I didn't like Ritz crackers much, but that is a lot of crackers and should last me a while. Whether I like them or not wasn't the objective at this point. Survival was my mission now.

I decided to put back the toilet paper, too. I could steal a roll from the clubhouse. Unbelievable. I can't believe I was planning on stealing, but it would give me a few extra dollars, and I doubt the clubhouse would suffer much with one less roll of toilet paper. I added it all up again. Yes. I had five extra dollars. I had a few slices of bread left but figured I would run out midweek, so I picked out a loaf of whole wheat and a can of chicken soup. I figured I could just eat the soup cold out of the can.

When the cashier was ringing up my items, a voice spooked me from behind, and I jumped. "What's up Country Club Girl?"

It was Langston in a soccer uniform. I flushed red and was totally taken off guard.

"Hey," I tried to sound calm, but my heart raced, and my throat was tight. "What are you doing here?"

Suddenly, thankful I had put the toilet paper and pads back.

He said, "I have a soccer game and stopped for Gatorade and snacks."

Langston's dad walked up behind him and smiled, "Hi Vivian."

The cashier was finished and said, "That will be $27.89."

Startled, I realized I had forgotten to add tax. How stupid could I be? Now I had to take an item off in front of Langston and his dad. Not very 'Country Club Girl.' I pulled $25 out of my backpack and awkwardly told the clerk to put back the bread.

Langston's dad quickly pulled out his wallet and said to the clerk, "I got this and handed her $3."

I was so embarrassed.

"Why are you shopping alone?" Langston asked.

Without making eye contact, I managed to say, "My dad is out of town and my mom has the flu." I nervously began assisting the elderly man bagging my groceries and was surprised at how fast I came up with the lie. Thank God I added the chicken soup. I quickly glanced at Langston and his dad. They appeared satisfied.

Langston's dad said, "I hope she feels better."

"Thank you. Good luck with your game," I stupidly uttered like a dumb cheerleader and rushed my cart filled with items out the door. I quickly snapped my helmet in place, grabbed my bags, and jumped on my bike, peddling fast to get around the corner of the store to readjust how to transport all this stuff back home. Thank God I parked my bike close. I just wanted to get away from Langston and his dad.

Why did I act so awkward? I am sure Langston thought I was a weirdo. I can't react so strange when I see people in public. Get it together, Vivian. Act normal. Act like your dad is a doctor. Act like your mom is shopping. Act like your mom didn't run away. Act like your dad didn't run away. Act like there is nothing wrong with your family.

Once out of view, I stopped and stuffed as much as I could in my backpack, leaving the bread and crackers in one plastic bag that I put in the bike basket.

A sudden rush of overwhelming panic and sadness swept over me. I rode home as fast as I could, trying not to cry. Please come home. *Mom. Dad. Please.* What if I run into someone next week? What excuse then? I can't do this. I can't act like nothing is wrong. Because everything is wrong. I need help. I can't survive all alone. I want mom to do the shopping. I don't want to pee in a bucket. I don't want to shower at the clubhouse. I'm not ready to do this. Tears blurred my vision on the last stretch of my ride home, but miraculously, I made it. Once I pulled up to the front door, I ran to the back, scaled the iron gate, flung open the French door, and flopped on the floor, letting the tears escape and my body release into sobs.

Chapter Twelve

After a mouse-sized lunch of four Ritz crackers topped with crunchy store brand peanut butter, I decided to go for another swim. I had to use the bathroom again anyway.

Once back home and feeling fresh, clean, and relieved of any bathroom needs, I began to read my history and English assignments before night engulfed me. Throwing myself into schoolwork helped me forget my situation.

For dinner, I ate a can of cold chicken noodle soup and indulged in eight Ritz crackers. Swimming was increasing my appetite, which wasn't good. I needed to come up with a way to make some money, so I could buy more food. I used to babysit a kid named Lucas in the neighborhood of townhouses next to our development, but without my phone, I couldn't call them and see if they needed any help. Maybe tomorrow I'll ride my bike over there and ask them.

As soon as the Sun was swallowed up by the Earth, blackness blanketed the house.

I hated the pitch darkness. I hated the silence. And now I had another thing to hate. The heat. It was April 29th, but it felt like July 1st right now. I dressed in the lightest cotton sleeveless t-shirt and shorts I could find and just laid on top of my sheets.

Why would mom leave? And dad, too? Why now, after months of lying on the couch, did Dad decide to go? It was such a bizarre coincidence that they would both leave on the same day, thinking I would be taken care of by the other.

In the black muggy silence, my mind searched for clues. I resurrected one of the last fights between my parents I could remember. It had been a while ago and mom did the yelling. Dad said very little—like always. Well, dad hadn't always been silent. Right after 'the incident', their fights were vicious on both sides, spewing insults that made my stomach jump and sent me to my room to put on headphones and crank my music. But over the last year and a half, the attacks came from Mom. She was still ready to fight. Dad sat mostly mute. He had given up.

On this one particular night, Mom ranted several minutes about bills and then I remember...... *Maybe I should just leave so you would be forced to get off the couch and get a job. Who cares what it is as long as it brings in some money? You could teach or go into research. There are options. Instead, you drink all day while I make peanuts as a clerk at a cheap department store, barely paying our bills.*

Dad, sounding dejected and depressed, finally replied, *No, I'm the one who should leave. You deserve better than me. You deserve someone who can buy you nice things, take you on trips, finish this house. No, no, I should go, so you can move on.*

They had fought the same version of this fight so many times over the last two years that I had tuned them out. They never followed through. However, I do remember one thing Mom added during this last fight that was different from the other battles. *Nothing changes if nothing changes.* That is what she said. I remember because her voice had shifted from energized anger to complete disgust and defeat, like she, too, was giving up. *Nothing changes if nothing changes.* The sheer disappointment deflated the statement like a balloon being let go before it was tied, fluttering around in the air, not knowing which way to go, before all the air was out, and it plopped on the floor.

I guess Mom decided to change....and so did Dad.... on the same day.

I wonder if either one of them thought about how leaving would affect me. I suppose each thought the other would take care of me. Now, no one was here to take care of me.

I had to take care of myself.

Chapter Thirteen

The next morning, I rode Mom's bike over to the gatehouse of the neighborhood across the street where the little boy, Lucas, and his parents, Mr. and Mrs. Rosen lived. I asked if I could go to their house, but the guard told me they moved.

Dejected, I circled my bike around the guard, and wheeled away. I was going to have to come up with another way to make money. Until then, no more than four Ritz crackers at a time.

Chapter Fourteen

Monday morning arrived, and I switched into Country Club Girl.

Wake at daybreak.

Go to clubhouse.

Swim.

Shower.

Blow dry hair.

I stared at my face in the mirror for any trace of desperation that might reveal my plight. Hair looks silky straight as usual. Thank God I decided not to get highlights last Christmas like Mom suggested. Why would she have wanted me to get highlights—a very expensive hair procedure—if she was struggling to pay our bills? I remember how excited she got when she asked if I wanted them—your hair is so perfect for highlights—thick, long, and amazing." I glanced at the prices on the wall and remembered the pawn shop incident and so many monotonous fights about money to know Mom couldn't afford this, and she wasn't being practical. I said, *maybe next year*, giving her a glimmer of hope, like a mother when they tell a toddler 'maybe,' knowing full well it is a 'no' but giving the child the idea there is a chance, so they don't throw a tantrum. But now, not being able to keep up with highlighted hair would be a visible clue of my second persona –pathetic, poor girl.

Thankfully, my hair looked like it always did. Country Club Girl on the outside. No one could tell the difference. I stared deep into my eyes reflecting back at me. Did they give anything away? Worry? Fear? Maybe. I don't know. I took a deep breath. Middle school kids don't look deep into anyone's eyes. Everyone is superficially surface. Fake. And for that, I am thankful. It helps me keep up my Country Club Girl image.

I wonder if Brianna, Bella, Sarah or Langston knew of my current state, they would still be my friends. I doubt it. They liked Country Club Girl. The girl who invited them to fancy lunches and lived in the fancy neighborhood and wore designer clothes. When I was with them, we rarely talked about anything meaningful. Everyone's head was usually in their phone, looking at whatever was currently trending. The way Langston called me Country Club Girl, was as if he was dating a 'thing' and not a real person. And why did I like being called Country Club Girl anyway? Stupid really. Maybe being a 'thing' right now is exactly what I wanted and needed. No need for anyone to look into my soul and discover my truth.

After that first time I invited Brianna, Bella, Sarah, Langston, Sterling, and Grady over to the clubhouse and I was officially christened 'Country Club Girl,' we started a routine of them coming over almost every weekend. Mom had just started our remodel. I brought everyone to our house when my room and Mom's room were finished. They all seemed impressed and told me how lucky I was. Brianna and Langston seemed particularly impressed with the enormous walk-in closets we both had and the designer clothes and shoes they housed.

But when 'the incident' happened, I stopped bringing everyone over to the house. Dad was always on the couch with a faint smell of stale wine. I had everyone just meet at the pool. I began giving excuses like 'the house is a construction zone, and no one is allowed' and 'mom wants to wait until the house is finished and do a big reveal.' These forced fabrications worked for a while and the gang seemed satisfied, but I was cognizant of the limited life of my lies. Time began to crawl into the future. People would start to get suspicious.

So, one weekend, when I knew I had reached my limit of lies, I nonchalantly said, 'I'm bored always going to our pool. Let's go to someone else's house next weekend. Brianna quickly said, 'Let's go to my house!' And with that simple declaration, our gatherings moved away from Royal Palm Estates. Brianna, Bella, and Sarah all lived in a neighborhood adjacent to the middle school called Live Oaks. Langston, Sterling, and Grady all lived in another neighborhood right next to Live Oaks called Hidden Oaks.

These two neighborhoods were giant planned communities with rows of houses that all looked alike and barely had a patch of grass to call a yard. Mom had taken me there the first weekend we decided to move our meet ups, and I remember her commenting 'Uhg, I could never live in a place like this with cheap, cookie-cutter houses.' I said nothing. The houses did all look alike and were cheaper looking than the grand homes of Royal Palm Estates, but Brianna's house was not a construction zone, and her dad had a job and wasn't drunk on the couch.

Brianna liked having everyone over to her house. When we all met there, we had fun. We played games and went down to their clubhouse, which also had a pool and was usually filled with kids and families. Towards the end of seventh grade, though, I felt increasingly uncomfortable going over there. Brianna started wanting to play games like 'spin the bottle' and 'truth or dare'. I didn't like these games, but everyone else seemed to, especially Langston and Brianna. He kept wanting to get me in a situation to kiss me.

The first time he accomplished his wish was on a 'spin the bottle' game. The bottle landed on Langston, and Brianna said he had to take me into the closet and kiss me. My heart went wildly out of control, and I hadn't imagined my first kiss would be in a closet with everyone giggling outside the door. My lips were shaking, and Langston aggressively thrust his tongue into my mouth and saliva smeared all around my lips. It felt cheap and disgusting. He said, 'relax' in a tone that had a hint of annoyance and a dominance I didn't like.

After that, I started making excuses not to go to Brianna's. Langston cornered me at school after a couple of missed weekends and asked me if anything was wrong. 'Didn't you like the kiss?' he demandingly asked. 'Yes,' I lied. 'I've just been busy.' I knew I would have to go over there again, or risk being excommunicated from the group and possibly lose my boyfriend. When I finally did go, I forced a few more kisses in the closet and pretended to like it to make Langston happy and not seem uncool. But I didn't like it. I hated it. I always imagined my first kiss to be more romantic, like on the beach at sunset, walking while holding hands and then stopping for a gentle kiss. Not some sloppy forced production to impress a group of people.

I snapped out of my unpleasant reverie. Now, Country Club Girl had to go to school to star in 'Pretend Everything is Perfect for Beachside Middle Schoolers.' A show I have been rehearsing for longer than I had realized.

Chapter Fifteen

"Do you still not have a phone?" Brianna asked.

"Yea, my parents are being crazy," I replied.

Before I could quickly change my least favorite topic on planet Earth—anything to do with my parents or home—she asked, "Can you come over this weekend?"

Bella, Langston, and Sarah plopped down at our lunch table just as I responded a quick, "No, I'm still grounded."

"What did you do to get grounded for this long?" asked Bella.

"You must have been a naughty girl," teased Langston.

"I talked back to my mom," I lied.

"God, I talk back to my mom all the time. I would never have a phone or leave the house if I lived with your parents," Brianna stated.

Everyone laughed.

"Your parents are being unreasonable. This is way too long to go without a phone. It is just not safe. What if you were abducted? They would never know where you were. My phone has Locate365 so my parents can find me at all times," Brianna stated.

"You might like that now, but when we get to high school, you won't," Langston winked at her as he said it. She smiled.

What just happened between them? Why the wink? What was with the smile? Something felt different.

Langston slid next to me and leaned in to get a whiff of my hair. "Your hair smells different. Did you change shampoos?"

"Yea," I was starting to feel uncomfortable.

"You need to go back to the old one. I liked it better," It was a command, and I didn't like it.

Ignoring him, I changed the subject. "Has anyone started the reading assignment for Mrs. Miller's class?"

"Uhg, I hate the classics. They are soooo hard to read and boring," Sarah replied.

I pulled out a peanut butter and jelly sandwich that I couldn't wait to eat. I was ravenous all the time since I began swimming twice a day. I had gotten sick of just peanut butter and added jelly this morning when making my lunch. The jelly had been in the refrigerator, but I didn't think jelly could spoil and gave it a little taste before making my sandwich. It had tasted good, so I slathered some on and now I wanted to devour it.

"Can I have your attention?" Vice Principal Kingsly was on stage with the microphone. The packed lunchroom of noisy eighth graders tried to settle down. I was thankful for the diversion.

Everyone turned to the stage to see a nicely dressed man in a crisp white shirt, red tie, and gray pants. He looked to be in his early forties and had a kind face that seemed like he was smiling even when he wasn't.

Next to him was a tall, naturally thin, and lanky looking kid, probably in high school, with caramel colored skin and wiry black hair that sort of purposely stuck out in every direction. He was cool looking, and the crowd settled quickly to hear what this opposite looking duo had to say.

"My name is Mr. Rexford, principal of Lorenzo Williams Technical High School, and I would like to tell you about us with the help of one of our students, Leo Lamont. We are a school of choice, meaning, instead of attending Gulfside High, you can apply to attend Lorenzo."

He started to go on and Langston twirled his eyes and said, "Yea, right, like I'm going to attend a tech school. That's where all the losers go."

The girls giggled at Langston's comment, but I thought he was rude.

"That Leo kid is gorgeous," Bella said.

Langston harrumphed, "If you like a Lorenzo loser. That is what everyone calls them at the high school."

Brianna, Bella, and Sarah giggled again.

I sat in silence.

I looked closely at Langston, his smug sneer slowly fading with his posse approval. My eyes penetrated every inch of him. Dirty brown hair, neatly slicked back. Pale pink polo shirt. Average brown eyes. Average height. Average intelligence. Average. And yet, he acted like he was the best thing to walk into the cafeteria. What did I like about him? His sense of humor? No. Not unless you like slightly offensive put down jokes. His compassion? No. Nonexistent. In the three years of dating him, I had never seen him help anyone. Fun to be around? No. Unless you like spin the bottle or endless conversations about soccer. Good kisser? Hardly. Wet slobber all over my face in a dark closet isn't the most romantic encounter. What was it then? I narrowed my eyes in a scrutinizing search for something I suddenly realized didn't exist.

Then, I glanced up to the stage where the kid that Langston just trashed was standing. I didn't know this kid at all, yet I could tell just by a distant glance, that there was more depth to him than Langston. There was a kindness in his expression that couldn't be faked. Langston was jealous.

Mr. Rexford was turning the microphone over to this Leo kid, but my group started talking about the end of year field trip to the water park, and I couldn't hear what he was saying. I ignored the whispered conversation at my table and tried to listen, but everyone around us took my group's cue that Leo and Mr. Rexford were irrelevant, signaling them to disregard this presentation, too. Soon, kids went back to finishing their lunches and talking.

Mr. Kingsly got back on the microphone and said, "If anyone is interested, take an application and a brochure. They will be back on May 19 for fall registration."

At this point no one was listening. Everyone was getting up to dump their trays and go to their afternoon classes.

Chapter Sixteen

"Today is May 1st and with state testing over, we will have one last project this month. We will read *The Prince and the Pauper* by Mark Twain and complete a choice board of project options," Mrs. Miller was explaining as she walked around the room passing out papers that gave directions to the choices.

"Now let me go over each choice. *The Prince and the Pauper* is historical fiction and is set during the time of King Henry the VIII. The story is about the king's son, Prince Edward, and a poor boy from London who looks just like the prince, and how they accidentally end up exchanging circumstances. The prince becomes the poor boy, and the poor boy becomes the prince. This is a fascinating period, and your first choice is to research this era, creatively illustrating the changes King Henry made to his kingdom that impacted history, his numerous wives and what happened to them, and what living at the King's court was like. Your next choice is to create a diary of Prince Edward as he journeys amongst the common man. Include at least ten journal entries. Your last choice is to pretend Prince Edward and the Pauper are able to correspond to one another via letter writing. Write at least three full page letters from each character explaining their situations and possible solutions to their problem. You must select one of these options. We will all be reading the book, some chapters together and some assigned. I want to help you get used to the vernacular of Mark Twain's writing. You may find it difficult at first, but you will get the hang of it. The project is due on May 19th."

She went on to give a brief overview of King Henry VIII and how he had six wives, Prince Edward being the son of the king's third wife, Jane Seymour. I decided to do the history project. I could go to the media center before school and use this project as an excuse not to go over to Brianna's for the next couple of weekends. My grounded lie would wear out soon.

When class was dismissed, Sarah, Bella, Brianna, Langston, and Sterling were all huddled in the hallway groaning about the project. "I hate the classics," whined Sarah again.

"Me, too," agreed Langston. The others all nodded, but I was looking forward to it and said nothing.

Once when I was little, my mom and I watched a documentary on King Henry VIII. Mom was so into it. I remember her gregarious giggling, her eyes bright and beautiful as she tried to explain things to me while watching. I was far too young to really understand the history part, but we both ooooed and ahhhed over the beautiful gowns. We shared buttery popcorn. It was a fun, memorable night. I remember thinking it was weird to have so many wives.

Now, I wanted to find out what happened to all of them. Mrs. Miller said that some wives were beheaded, but she wouldn't go further than that because she wanted those of us who were selecting the history choice to do the research. What horrible thing could a wife do to earn a beheading?

But more than wanting to research the history of King Henry VIII, I wanted to read the story. *The Prince and the Pauper.* A story of identity confusion. A story about a poor boy playing the part of a rich prince. A story about a rich prince playing the part of a poor boy. How did the pauper boy act when people thought he was the prince? Did it change him? Did he become spoiled and arrogant? Did he try to retain his newfound royal status at any cost? How did Prince Edward manage when he was thrust into the pauper's life? Did he whine and cry and carry on? Did he try to convince people he was actually a prince? Did he become a beggar in the street?

I wanted to know.

Chapter Seventeen

After Mrs. Miller's class, I had math then study hall. Kids with straight A's in sixth and seventh grade earned last period study hall in eighth grade. There weren't many of us and no one from my group. There was a small room connected to the media center designated for study hall students. It was quiet and dark and private, and I loved it. Most of the eighth graders there were taking a high school class online to get ahead. Six computers flanked one wall, and I immediately went to one that wasn't occupied and started my research on King Henry VIII and Tudor history. I asked Mrs. Brooks, the media specialist, if there were any books on King Henry the VIII and that time period. A few minutes later, she emerged with three books. I checked them out and flipped through one, glancing at the colored pictures.

Towards the end of study hall, my stomach started to cramp. I looked at the clock and noticed I only had five minutes before the dismissal bell. There was no time to use the bathroom before getting on the bus. Besides, the bathrooms were locked before the bell rang anyways due to some students' 'nefarious behavior' according to administration.

The cramping was getting worse.

On the bus ride home, I had to bend over and hold my stomach. Why was this happening? Then I remembered the jelly. Can jelly spoil? It tasted fine. Or maybe my taste buds were 'off' because I was so hungry all the time.

No one from my group rode the bus. Thank God they all walked home. I usually read on the bus and relished the silence from all the phony chatter of the day.

"Are you OK?" a girl I barely recognized asked.

"Yea," I uttered. But I wasn't fine. I was concentrating on not having diarrhea on the bus.

Just a few more minutes, and I would be home. But when the bus lurched to a stop and I raced down the steps to run towards the clubhouse, Winston stopped me and said, "You can't go to the pool right now, Vivian. The locker room and pool are closed for remodeling. It's going to be closed for two-three weeks."

"Ok, thanks," I said trying to appear normal. I couldn't think about how devastating this news was right now because I was about to poop my pants.

I managed to get around to the courtyard where I had been scaling the iron gate each day but knew I couldn't climb without crapping in my pants. I slunk behind a hedge, out of sight, and hurriedly pulled down my jeans and let everything go. I had a mixed feeling of primal bodily relief and sudden horror. What was happening to my life? Pooping behind bushes like an animal?? I didn't have anything to wipe so I took some leaves and prayed they wouldn't give my ass a rash.

I pulled up my pants and crawled away from the dung heap. I looked back for a brief moment and decided to cover up my mess, like a cat in a litterbox. Humiliated, I scaled the iron gate and let myself into the house. Dropping to the floor, I curled up in a fetal position and began to cry.

A new panic suddenly set in.

No shower or bathroom for two or three weeks. What was I going to do now?

Chapter Eighteen

After scrubbing my hands with soap and water following the outdoor bathroom fiasco, I had half a gallon of water left in the plastic jug. Hardly enough to bathe and drink.

When night finally took over the sky, I grabbed two empty jugs I found in the garage and stuffed them into my backpack, scaled the iron gate, and slipped behind a couple of houses to cut over to the pool. I wanted to stay out of sight of the guard house and off the street so no one could see me.

I ducked under the yellow tape marking off the construction zone. There, before me, was an empty pool. Workers had chipped all the tiles off the lip and stacks of concrete debris encircled the cavernous shell. It looked like a larger version of my pool at home. I tried the doors to the locker room, but they were locked. I walked around the clubhouse building and saw another building that housed golf carts. I had never been over there. As discreetly as I could, I walked all the way around the building and saw what I was looking for: a water fountain. I got out my jugs and filled them with water and put them back into my backpack. Then I looked down and saw a water spigot with a coiled green hose attached. I could come here and take quick showers with the water hose, but that would be risky. Someone could see me. I'm sure cameras captured images all over this area. I was probably being recorded now. I needed to be swift and savvy so no one could recognize me, even if they saw an image on screen.

Then I thought about one of the houses I ran behind to get here. All their hurricane shutters were closed, so I knew they were snowbirds gone for the season. I wondered if they left their water running or shut it off for the summer?

On my way back home, I searched the perimeter of the shutter house and found what I was looking for: a water spigot. It didn't have a green hose attached. They probably took it off and put it in their garage for the summer. I turned the knob. Water came rushing out. I could just shove my body under it but that looked pretty hard to do. There was just enough room to wash my feet. Or I could get our hose and attach it for just two weeks.

The spigot was hidden behind a hedge. This could work temporarily.

I hurried home and unloaded my jugs of water and then went outside to find our hose. I unscrewed it, which was harder than I thought. I crept quietly back to the shutter house and screwed on the hose. I had forgotten to bring shampoo, so I raced back. I changed into a bathing suit- briefly thinking about the one I left in the clubhouse locker that was probably in a trash can now, grabbed a towel and wrapped my shampoo in it. I scuttled back to the shutter house and did the quickest cold shower, crouched behind the bushes.

I walked back slowly and thought how dark and quiet this neighborhood was. When my parents decided to move here, I hated it. We had left a nice little house that wasn't large, but it had charm and there were a few families in the neighborhood. It had life. This place was like a cold dark palace with only one princess occupant. But right now, I relished the desolation and vacancy of Royal Palm Estates. I didn't want anyone to see me having to defecate and shower in the bushes.

When I got home, I collapsed on my bed and stared at my ceiling. A whiff of my hair caught my nose. Well, my hair smelled like my shampoo at least. Langston will like that. No generic country club shampoo for a while. But I had no hair dryer. I would have to let it air dry. He will most likely comment about that. Right now, I was too tired to care.

My stomach grumbled with hunger, but I was afraid to eat. I still didn't feel quite right after my diarrhea explosion. I was exhausted but couldn't sleep. My mind went back to fourth grade when Mrs. McHarris read *Charlotte's Web* to us. She stopped at a part when Wilbur was worried he would be killed, *"When your stomach is empty and your mind is full, it's always hard to sleep."* Most kids weren't really paying attention to Mrs. McHarris. They just wanted to get on with the story because she had promised we could see the movie afterward and eat popcorn. I remembered it though. Because there was a distant look in Mrs. McHarris' eyes that said she related to that sentence, and I had wondered what was going on in her life. I felt the urge to hug her after she stopped reading that day. She squeezed me back and smiled.

Wilbur was right. It *is* hard to sleep when you are hungry. It *is* hard to sleep when you are scared. It *is* hard to sleep when your mind is full of questions about your survival.

I reached for the flashlight I kept on my nightstand and clicked it on, pointing it straight up. I had a sudden urge not to be in the dark. A roach scuttled across the ceiling. My little friend. I hadn't seen him since the last time I turned on the flashlight. I wonder if he was searching for water. Or food maybe? Or his family? Was he lost or abandoned? Had his family left him?

Normally, I would freak out about a roach in the house. That was one thing my mom and I had in common. We first started spotting them six months after the construction of our remodel came to a halt. They weren't those giant palmetto bugs northerners always said were roaches. Mom used to tell me those bugs weren't nearly as scary as the smaller, lighter brown German roaches. German roaches meant you most likely have an infestation. A large palmetto bug just means it rained a lot and one got in the house. Mom promptly called an exterminator to get rid of them. She said to me, 'I can put up with a stalled construction zone, but not roaches.' Maybe she had seen the return of the German roaches and that is why she left.

I wonder how many more are out there.

Something tickled the back of my neck, and I sat up a little. I slowly reached under my damp hair and pressed down until I felt a crunch. Instinctively grasping something, I closed my hand into a fist, squeezing slightly. I opened, and there was a brown roach the size of a lima bean. I didn't jump up and scream. I didn't freak out. I didn't really care. The roaches were back.

I guess mom stopped paying the exterminator, too.

Chapter Nineteen

It didn't take long for the middle school court to make fun of my hair. I exited the bus and began my usual walk across the center courtyard, when Langston, Sterling, Grady, Sarah, Bella, and Brianna were huddled, laughing at something. Langston looked up from the group and almost looked away as if he saw a nobody but then did a double take.

"What the hell?" he gaped.

Everyone turned to stare at me. Brianna stifled a snotty snicker. The others just looked bewildered. I squared my shoulders and inhaled bravery.

"Like my new look?" I faked confidence that deserved an Oscar. Before leaving, I studied my wild main of hair in the mirror. I didn't think it looked bad. Untamed. Out-of-control. But freely framing my face. I decided I liked it.

"I hate it," snarled Langston.

The others followed his lead.

"Yea, I like it smoother. Like before," added Brianna.

"You need to change it back to normal tomorrow," demanded Langston and added, "You look like a homeless person."

Everyone laughed. I didn't. I liked my hair. I liked it more and more with each disapproving comment and scrutinizing look, and I wasn't going to change it. Period. Even if I had access to electricity and could blow dry my hair into silk, I decided that this was my new look. One that Langston hated. One that Brianna hated. One that made me look like a homeless person. One that I suddenly loved.

The bell rang and we all scattered to our first period.

For the next two and a half weeks, I dove into my literature assignment. I became fascinated with King Henry's wives and their court. How one group would fall out of favor with the king and another group would be in the wings waiting to rise in social standing and power. I was particularly interested in Anne Boleyn and Catherine Parr, the two queens that seemed to have the courage to stand up to the king. The former ended up with her head in a basket. The latter survived.

The king's first wife, Mary, was not producing a male heir to the throne of England. After many miscarriages, she had only produced a daughter, named Mary as well. She was a Spanish princess and a devout Catholic and Europe was experiencing many religious reforms to the Catholic Church. This upset the devout Catholics and religious tensions were mounting throughout Europe.

Anne Boleyn was part of a family of reformers to the Catholic Church. She caught the eye of the King, who was upset about not having a son, and she began a plot to be the next Queen of England. She was brilliant, beautiful, and believed in religious reform. She convinced King Henry that she could produce a male heir for him and that the reason Mary couldn't was because God was punishing him. Mary had been the wife of his older brother, Arthur, who died shortly after Arthur and Mary were betrothed. Anne had the king convinced he should never have married his brother's wife. The only way to get divorced from Mary was to break away from the Catholic church, where divorce was not allowed.

King Henry and Anne did marry, but Queen Anne only produced one girl as well, Elizabeth. Anne was beheaded for apparently being a witch and casting a spell-- with her seductive beauty, intelligence, and wit-- on the King to divorce his first wife, Mary-the regal

Spanish princess, sending a country into a religious revolution.

After Mary, now sent to live her days in a remote castle away from the fashionable Tudor court, and Anne, now in a grave, King Henry married a woman who was the opposite of Anne in every way—quiet, demur, no opinions but those of the King's—Jane Seymour. She died giving birth to the son the King longed for, Prince Edward. This is the prince the story we were reading, *The Prince and the Pauper* by Mark Twain, is about. After the tragic death of Jane, the King was convinced by his advisors to marry a German princess named Anne of Cleves, but that marriage was annulled (pretend it never happened) due to the King not finding her attractive enough. Like his first wife, Mary, Anne of Cleves was sent to live in a distant castle.

Next, he married the dim-witted, but supposedly beautiful and fun—and very young-- Catherine Howard, the cousin to Anne Boleyn. She cheated on the King, and he had her beheaded. The Howard girls were an unlucky bunch.

The last wife, Catherine Parr, was a widower when the king met her. Beautiful, intelligent, also wanting religious reform like Anne Boleyn, but older and wiser to the ways of the luxurious and dangerous Tudor court. Unlike Anne, she learned how to help the country reform Christianity in a way that didn't offend the King and get her accused of witchcraft and beheaded. She is the only queen that wasn't beheaded or divorced from the king.

For my assignment, I decided to create a Tudor family tree, like one I found on the internet during study hall. I had the media specialist make a copy of it so I could take it home and finish the project.

Once home, I spread out my art supplies on the concrete floor in the living room. I loved to draw and added castles, the English countryside, and images of the lavish Tudor court. I also added a platform, executioner, and a bloody head rolling into a basket, which was sort of fun, and I got a little too into this image. When I stood back and analyzed my artwork, the grotesque, bloody head sort of dominated the assignment. The courtyard surrounding the guillotine looked a lot like the courtyard at Beachside Middle School, and the bloody head had wild, untamed hair that I recognized from the mirror.

Then a roach came out of nowhere and scurried across the bloody head. I shooed it off the poster board. Picking up two different shades of brown, I added a drawing of a tiny German roach running along the ground where Anne's head was about to land in the basket.

I was so busy with this project that I didn't have time to think about Langston's rude comments about my wild, untamed hair, which grew more annoying every day. About my problems at home: no electricity. no water. dwindling funds. I didn't have time to think about eating peanut butter every day. About the increasing number of German roaches. About the increasing darkness, silence, heat. About the increasing loneliness.

I was so busy that I was oblivious to the rising social groups lurking in the corners of the middle school courtyard, waiting to publicly see my head roll into a basket.

Chapter Twenty

"You need a new lunchbox," Brianna claimed. "That thing is disgusting."

She was right. I knew it. Mom had gotten it for me before sixth grade started. Before 'the incident'. It was a trendy name brand at the time and five times the cost of a regular lunchbox. Everyone had wanted one just like it and soon, all the sixth-grade girls, wanting to be just like Country Club Girl, were forcing their parents to buy them overpriced lunchboxes.

But now, almost three years later, my once adorable lunchbox was pathetic looking. The stitching had frayed along the handle from too many washes and overuse. I tried to trim off the threads, but new threads began to unravel at even greater speed. The fabric had faded, and faint stains were still visible. At first the stains were hard to spot because of the lunchbox's colorful pattern. For the first two years, I used Oxy Clean to get them out and it worked pretty well, but we haven't had Oxy clean in the house for over a year and the stains had grown darker and more recognizable. I looked at Brianna's lunchbox and suddenly noticed it wasn't like mine at all. I didn't recognize the brand, but it was beautiful with blue and yellow flowers and bright green leaves. Then I noticed Bella and Sarah's lunchbox. They were almost identical. Different flowers, but definitely the same brand. When did everyone get new lunchboxes?

I just mumbled, "Yea, I do need a new lunchbox."

Quietly, I unzipped my piece of junk. Langston pushed his way between Brianna and me. "Move over ladies." His posse appeared behind him and circled around the table to sit across from us, next to Sarah and Bella.

He looked straight at me and said, "When are you going to change your hair?" There was such disapproving disgust to his tone. "You look like an alley cat." He snickered and so did his entourage.

Brianna added, "It really isn't a good look for you."

I was thinking of a response as I pulled my peanut butter, minus the jelly, sandwich out of my lunchbox, when a German roach quickly crawled out, escaping down the side and onto the table so fast, I didn't have time to think or do anything.

I froze.

Brianna screamed first followed by Sarah and Bella.

Langston leapt to his feet, leaving his lunch on the table. Everyone sprung to their feet.

Except me.

I just sat there,

unmoving,

paralyzed.

A second roach emerged out of a small, worn-out hole in the bottom corner of the tattered lunchbox.

More screams.

A crowd had formed. Hysterical screams mixed with laughter lured more spectators.

And as if all the pandemonium had woken the dormant army of German roaches, hundreds began to swarm out and scurry every direction across the table.

I finally stood in slow motion, watching my fake Country Club Girl façade evaporate before my eyes. I felt a couple of roaches crawl down my arm and several crawl down my back.

Someone yelled, "Gross, look!" pointing at me as the bugs scurried down my body.

The crowd had pulled out their phones and were recording the entire scene, loudly laughing and pointing and running around each other to get out of the way of the swarm which had now reached the floor, sending roaches and kids every direction.

Some aimed their video weapons at me as their phones recorded the horror, while others captured the swarm on the table and floor.

I turned and walked out of the cafeteria, not even caring that roaches were escaping my body, leaving a trail of truth.

***

All bathrooms were locked during lunch, except the one in the cafeteria. So, seeking refuge in a bathroom was not an option. When I was out of sight of the cafeteria, I managed to brush off any remaining stubborn roaches still trying to cling to my clothes.

I slipped up to the second floor to go to the media center. Chess club. Book club. It was where the "geek squad" went for lunch. The media center was usually open to these clubs only, but I could try.

When I rounded the corner, the door to the media center was wide open with a man I sort of recognized standing as a door stopper. Next to him in the hallway was a tall kid who looked like a high school student. I vaguely recognized him, too. The Lorenzo Loser Assembly. Then I remembered the last thing Mr. Kingsly said as the disinterested crowd dispersed during that lunch presentation. They were coming back to register students.

I slowed down my pace, preparing a composed interchange when a kid I didn't know walked by and said, "Hey, you're roach girl."

I stopped, startled. "What?"

He showed me his phone. Someone had sent out a video on snapchat with me just sitting at the lunch table with roaches crawling everywhere. The caption read, *Roach Girl*. The snapchat sent by: Brianna Dunn.

May 19. Today was May 19th.

Nearly 500 years ago on this very day, Anne Boleyn was executed at the desire of a tyrannical King by the sharp blade of a medieval hatchet. Her head rolling for all to see. She had fallen from his grace, for made up reasons, so a new group – a new girl—could rise in favor.

My hatchet: a smart phone.

My executioner: Brianna and probably the whole gang along with middle school vultures feasting on a fabulous meal of misfortune.

My new title: Roach Girl.

Well, goodbye Country Club Girl. The roach is out of the bag.

Chapter Twenty-one

"Hi, I'm Mr. Rexford, principal of Lorenzo Williams Technical School and this is Leo Lamont, a sophomore studying carpentry and project management. Are you here to register?" The principal smiled hopefully, wearing a white polo shirt with LWTHS logo and khaki pants.

I tried not to stare at the Leo kid who stood quietly with a kind, confident expression, but it was hard. He was the most interesting looking guy I'd ever seen. He was a melting pot of United Nation races, giving him his own country. His skin was silky smooth and the color of melted caramel chocolate. His eyes were crystal blue, and he didn't take them off mine, which a bit disarming. I had never seen a person with dark skin and light blue eyes, and I guess that made it hard for me to look away, too. I wonder why he was staring at me. Did

I have a lingering roach crawling up my neck? I nonchalantly touched my skin to be sure.

For a moment, I forgot all about the roaches and what had just happened to me. The color of his eyes made me think of the pool at the clubhouse where I had been swimming to cool myself and forget my problems. I think I began holding my breath, like I was under water, as I continued to stare. I uncomfortably shifted my eyes away and glanced at his wiry, wild hair sticking up in every direction, but with purpose and unconventional style. He stood a lanky head taller than Mr. Rexford and moved with ease, unlike the gawky motions of most middle schoolers.

Knowing this was my only escape from the humiliating cafeteria scene I just unintentionally caused, I quickly asked, "Could I get some more information?"

"Sure!   Come this way," Mr. Rexford enthusiastically left his post and Leo followed.

He sat me down at a table with a trifold presentation board decorated with pictures, highlighting programs the school offered.

At first, I pretended to be interested to hide from my rapidly descending fall from grace, but as I stared at the brochure, something caught my eye.

Electrician. Plumber. Carpenter. Architectural draftsman.

Mr. Rexford immediately launched into a pitch for their medical programs, "We have the best surgical nursing program in south Florida. Hospitals all over the nation want our surgical nursing students."

I blurted out, "I'm more interested in the electrician and plumbing programs. And carpentry."

Mr. Rexford was caught off guard for just a moment, but picked right up, "Ok, we don't get many girls in this program." I knew he didn't mean to sound sexist. He was just being honest. I hadn't seen many female plumbers either.

Leo was giving me a hard stare, probably wondering if I was mocking the school.

But when I seriously started asking questions, Leo's face softened back up. "I don't understand how this works. I'm supposed to go to Gulfside High School. That is where my bus will take me next year," I began.

Before I could continue, Mr. Rexford jumped in, "Lorenzo is a school of choice, meaning you fill out an application and you must be accepted. Last year we had nearly 1,000 students apply, but we only accept 150 each year. If you are accepted, the bus will pick you up no matter where you live. Next Friday is the deadline for applications. We are a technical high school, so we offer trade skills as well as normal academic subjects. You select the first three programs you are interested in on your application." He paused and looked at me with the nicest face and continued, "No one applies to our school from the north side of town, and I don't think we have ever had a student from Beachside Middle come to Lorenzo. We really want a variety of students from all areas of town represented at our school. And if you really want plumbing or carpentry, or the electrical program, I am sure you would get in. You will probably be the first female in the building trades and the only one on your bus from the north side of town. Where exactly do you live?"

I reluctantly uttered, "Royal Palm Estates."

"You will definitely be the only one on your bus," he said. "And I would love to have more students coming to Lorenzo from this side of town."

Suddenly, my head started racing, and I forgot all about Roach Girl. I liked the idea of being the first female in a program, and the first person from the north side of town to attend a trade school.

"Most of our students really know what they want to do with their life. Do you *really* know what you want to do?" he asked, unsure of my atypical inquiries into plumbing and electrical work.

I wanted to answer, *Survive. That is what I want to do. Survive.* I really hadn't given any thought to my career. My only concerns up to this point in my life were wearing the right clothes, having the right hair, and maintaining my Country Club status with my friends. But as I stared at the brochure and looked at the pictures on the presentation board, what began as a spontaneous, desperate decoy from the humiliating cafeteria scene, now turned into genuine interest.

How shallow were my previous preoccupations? How dumb? What I was looking at now was reality. Something I needed to get me out of my stagnant, sad situation.

"Mr. Rexford, I really want to know how a house is built. Every aspect of it from plumbing to electrical to carpentry. I want to be a builder. A remodeler. That is what I want to do." As the words escaped my lips, I breathed life into a possible career. I suddenly knew this is what I needed to do. Just like a bird knows it is supposed to fly or an abandoned girl knows she is supposed to survive.

I glanced over at Leo. Was that amusement or was he impressed?

Mr. Rexford's expression changed, too. His momentary uncertainty turned into renewed excitement, "Yes, that is great. We need more girls in these trades."

He smiled and handed me an application. "Fill this out tonight and have your parents sign it. Then bring it to your guidance counselor Monday, and she will send it to us."

Mr. Rexford shook my hand, smiled, and said, "We hope to see you at Lorenzo Williams Technical School."

I was about to become a Lorenzo Loser, and I couldn't wait.

Chapter Twenty-two

I wanted to skip Mrs. Miller's English class. I didn't want to face my friends, but I had to turn in my assignment. I specifically didn't want to face Brianna. I knew she had started the viral video with the complete purpose of humiliating me. Her sudden turn on me was perplexing. Or maybe it wasn't? I was so overwhelmed surviving, that I had distanced myself from her and everyone really. I didn't talk to anyone on the phone. I didn't hang out with anyone on weekends. The only time I saw the gang was at school. They may have been plotting against me for weeks. I wouldn't know.

Overt snickering and whispering trailed from mobs of eighth graders as I passed to my locker to get my poster and then over to Mrs. Miller's room. Just before I reached the classroom door, a hand grabbed my arm. I turned to face Langston.

"Hey can we talk?" He asked.

"Class starts in like two minutes," I answered back. The sound of his voice now repulsed me.

"It's quick," he pulled me off to a corner of the hallway. "I think we need to break up. I have been wanting to call you, but you haven't had a phone and you never come over to Brianna's anymore. I was going to tell you at lunch today, but it was a little rowdy." He looked at the floor.

I stared at him, but he was too much of a coward to stare back or maybe he just couldn't stand to look at my hair. I wondered if everything he said was a lie, and he was just so grossed out by the roaches and everyone making fun of me, that it turned him off. That *I* turned him off. I suddenly felt like King Henry's fifth wife, Anne of Cleves. She had been from Germany and King Henry's advisors thought the match would be good for an alliance with the country. He hadn't really seen her until the wedding. When he finally did see her, he hated her looks and wasn't attracted to her at all. He quickly sent her to live in a castle. Imagine casting someone off that you don't really know because you don't like their looks. At least she didn't get beheaded.

Two months ago, this breakup may have devastated me. But right now, I felt indifferent, relieved actually. My disdain towards Langston—and everyone in the group--had been growing for weeks. I didn't relate to them anymore. My problems were too big for their little lives. Yes, I am relieved Langston broke up with me. One less thing to worry about. I bet Anne of Cleves was relieved, too. Off to live in isolation, free from any worry of being executed for doing or saying the wrong thing.

"I agree." Is all I said.

I turned, walked straight into class, and sat at the empty seat next to a kid I didn't know at all. He mumbled 'hi,' and I uttered 'hi' back. I was suddenly embarrassed that I didn't even know this kid's name. I had been in class with him all year and wouldn't have recognized him on the street. Had I been so self-centered that I barely knew anyone other than my group?

Brianna walked in a minute later with Langston. The two of them sat together at the table where Langston and I usually sat.

Then it hit me. Langston never really liked me. He liked Country Club Girl. He told me he was in love with me a week after he first came to my house before sixth grade. Love? Really? How stupid that seemed now. And I believed him. I remember liking that he said he loved me. I felt a rush of importance. I felt special. Brianna, Sarah, and Bella had gushed over my rehashing of those romantic words, making me feel even more special and more grown up than the others. I was the first to be told 'I love you' by a boy. The funny thing was I had had a hard time saying it back to him. The words felt awkward when I forced them out. Like it was the polite thing to do to repeat them back to him. How did I know whether I loved him or not? I knew him from elementary school, but I didn't *really* know him. Nor did he know me- *really* know me. He just knew that I lived in a fancy neighborhood and ate fancy French fries.

He liked Country Club Girl. I see that clearly now. He wouldn't be caught dead with Roach Girl.

And Brianna was no better. They were made for each other. Brianna had been my best friend since third grade. She was fun to be around and in elementary school, we were inseparable. Brianna slept over a lot in the fifth grade when we lived in our old house. I loved my elementary school days, when the world was full of Littlest Pet Shop toys, Disney movies, Legos, and karaoke singing. When I lived in a cute yellow house with white shutters and window boxes filled with blue and white flowers. When my parents smiled. When the fridge was full. When the electricity worked and the water came out of the faucet. When the only roach I encountered was outside.

Brianna humiliating me hurt more than Langston breaking up with me.

I remember mom telling me once after Brianna slept over that she was a 'climber.' Mom sounded sort of snobby, and I asked her what that meant. She told me a climber is someone who desires popularity and a higher social status than what they were born into. I silently didn't agree with my mom at that time but said nothing. I hated it when mom said stuff like that. She often acted superior to others, and it was embarrassing. I wanted to add, *'Aren't you a climber?'* but resisted that too. I guess when you are higher on the climb, you forget your beginnings.

But thinking about Brianna and our friendship made me wonder...*How close could we really be? How close was our friendship really? If it was special, wouldn't I have confided to her when my dad operated on the wrong eye of a patient causing him to lose his medical license and lay on the couch all day depressed? Wouldn't I have told her we were out of money and living in a shell of a house, barely able to pay our bills? Wouldn't I have told her my mom left....and my dad, too.... on the same day? Was I afraid of her reaction? Was I afraid she would dump me as a friend? Was I afraid she would tell people and embarrass me? Was I afraid Bella and Sarah would do the same thing?*

Yes.

That is exactly what I was afraid of. Maybe deep down I knew my mom was right about Brianna. She was a social climber, waiting for me to fall so she could step in, only interested in my friendship because my dad was a doctor, my mom a socialite living a fancy life, and these connections helped her rise.

What did my not telling her I was living alone, eating peanut butter and roach sandwiches, defecating behind hedges, taking garden hose showers behind bushes say about me? Was my unwillingness to share and be authentic a sign that I was no better than her or any of them—Bella, Sarah, Langston? Trying to keep up the lie? Pretending to be Country Club Girl? Liking it? Did that make me just as much of a phony as a social climber?

Middle school had started off even better than elementary school. Ruling the school like the fashionable crowd at King Henry's court. But as my home life got worse, my attempts to make everything appear normal tugged at my conscience. I was always switching from school me to home me. It gradually wore me down. It had affected Brianna's and my relationship, and I didn't really get it until now.

Mom had been right. Brianna was a climber. And I was a willing participant, like an accomplice to a crime. Just as guilty. But if I wanted to suddenly become authentic and confess the real me, Brianna and the gang were the last people I trusted.

I trusted no one.

I was completely and utterly alone.

No mother.

No father.

No friends.

Chapter Twenty-three

I managed to shove my way through the masses of students exiting the school at dismissal, trying to block out the jeers of 'Roach Girl', snickers, points, and outright laughter by the boldest and most heartless middle schoolers. I actually liked the bold 'in your face' comments and laughter. If you are going to be a jerk, own it and let me know your true colors. These kids were at least brave, and I can respect brave. Not like the cowards that whispered behind my back or tried to cover their mouths while they quietly exchange insults. I have no respect for them. Pretenders. Like the vultures at King Henry's court plotting secretly behind Queen Anne's back to bring her down and destroy her.

But didn't Queen Anne deserve her fate? Didn't she destroy Queen Mary in her quest to become queen? Didn't she plot and scheme her way to the throne? Did I deserve dethroning? I didn't destroy anyone. I was the one being destroyed. But I was faking my country club status. For what? To be part of a shallow, phony clique that I didn't even like anymore. I bet as Queen Anne walked towards her execution, the crowds shouted 'witch' and other offensive jeers. "Hey, Roach Girl!" echoed all around me. I read that Anne held her head high as she walked to her fate. As I walked through the loud, rowdy crowd, I tried so hard to do the same.

They can say whatever they want. They can kick me out of the middle school court. I don't care. Who wants to be Country Club Girl? Not me.

I made it to the bus, and it was no better there. Kids made rude comments and acted like they didn't want to sit by me. Like more roaches were going to crawl out of my shirt which grossed them out and made me a pariah.

Just get me home. Staring out the bus window, my mind went to King Henry's last wife, Catherine Parr. She was a reformer of the Catholic church like Anne, but she had survived. Vultures wanted to bring her down, too, like Anne, but she outwitted them.

I wonder how she did it? How did she survive the brutal Tudor court? How would I survive these last days of brutal middle school?

I started imagining Roach Girl like a superhero. Indestructible. A survivor of the dinosaur era. Able to withstand being stepped on. Living through The Big Bang. The Ice Age. Middle School.

Country Club Girl was weak. She pretended.
Roach Girl didn't just survive. She thrived.
Which girl would I rather be?
Roach Girl.

Chapter Twenty-four

When I got home, I filled out my application for Lorenzo Williams Technical High School. I listed Electrical, Plumbing, and Carpentry as my top three choices for programs. I knew this was probably a hopeless dream, but the fantasy of fixing this house filled my brain. My parents had cowardly folded when dealt a bad poker hand and left the mess for someone else to fix. *What if that someone was me? What if I did what they couldn't do?*

I studied all the programs offered at this school. The school Langston called a place for losers. Boat and Yacht mechanic; aircraft pilot and mechanic; nurse technician; dental technician; welding; carpentry; plumbing; electrical; digital design; computer technician. Why would Langston and the kids at Gulfside High call these people losers? As far as I could see, these programs were more interesting and meaningful than the useless crap I was being forced to ingest at Beachside Middle School.

I forged Mom's name at the bottom of the application without one ounce of remorse that forgery was bad. After all, wasn't leaving your child to survive on her own a worse crime? Mom justified her actions by telling herself she was leaving me with dad, but she and I both knew that was the same as leaving me alone. Dad was useless. And she knew it. How could she leave me with a depressed drunk? The burden she felt trying to take care of both of us was double for me. I have no job and am 13 years old. How did she really expect me to handle all of this? Did she really think dad would miraculously get off the couch and suddenly get a job without her there? Well....... he did get off the couch, but where he went was a mystery. He didn't go get a job and take care of me. Neither one of them chose me over their own selfish feelings. So, forging my mom's name was simple. Who would find out? No one.

I was starving, having had no food at lunch today. I went to make myself a peanut butter sandwich and when I opened the bread, a roach crawled out. I jumped, startled, and then my heart sank. I threw the bread in the trash. Then I stopped and looked at the bag in the trash. Almost an entire loaf. What if I ran out of money and food? So what if a tiny roach crawled out. I reached back in the trash and fetched the loaf of bread. I pulled a few slices out to see if there were other roaches. When I got about halfway through my examination, another roach scurried across the counter. I kept going. Another. Then another. Once all of them were released from the bag, I debated. *Should I throw the slices away or not?* I couldn't believe I was contemplating this. But I was. I rummaged through the one old cabinet we left sitting in the kitchen after the demolition, looking for Tupperware containers. I found a large one with a tight-fitting lid. I put all the slices into it, except two, and sealed the lid. I opened the peanut butter and pretended I never saw a roach.

Somewhat satisfied, I had to face the hard truth that I needed a way to make money. The $100 Target gift card I was going to get for perfect attendance and the cash I had would eventually run out and then what would I do? I thought of asking the guidance counselor if I could apply for free lunch, but that would alert those nosy counselors. They would swoop in and realize what was happening and put me in foster care. And that would be bad. At least I think it would be bad. All the stories I read about a kid going into foster care, ends with some horrific tragedy and them escaping and running away. Then I would be living under a tree or bridge somewhere.

Can't risk that. So, I had to make some money, somehow.

***

The remodel of the clubhouse pool and locker rooms was taking longer than two weeks, and I was still waiting until dark to slink over to the shutter house and perform my garden hose shower ritual. I didn't mind it that much because the rush of cold water felt so good on my sweaty skin. My math teacher, Mr. Mason, said it was the hottest May in history and was going to be the hottest summer on record. With no electricity, I felt hot, sticky, and gross all the time. *Was Florida ever not hot?* I had the sudden urge to hop on a bus and move to Alaska. But that was unrealistic because one, I had no money for bus fare, two, I had no money for a coat and boots, and three, I had no money for food and a place to stay once I got there.

Money. It was always about not having enough money. I hated money. But I needed money. That made me hate it more.

What I couldn't get used to was using the bucket and the outside hedge as my bathroom. Crouching down and pooping made me feel like a stray dog. Humiliating. I couldn't wait for the pool and clubhouse to reopen. I usually pooped before I performed the garden hose shower. It washed the humiliation off me.

Once back in my house, I slipped on the coolest thing I owned and laid on top of my covers, brainstorming ways to make money. I was one of the youngest kids in my grade level and turned 14 on July 23. You had to be sixteen to have a real job. Babysitting was out. I didn't want mothers catching a whiff of my situation, and they might, if they say something like, 'Let me talk to your mom.' Or 'I'll pick you up at your house.' Can't have that.

Then I had an idea. I remembered the day Mom left I ran into her closet to see what she had taken with her. I was encouraged that she wouldn't be gone long because it looked like she didn't take much, and my mother loved her clothes, shoes, and jewelry. Her luggage was gone and whatever she could fit in it, but my mom was a shopaholic. She had clothes with the tags still on and shoes barely, if ever worn. And most of her stuff was still here.

I grabbed my flashlight and went over to her enormous walk-in closet to do some inventory. Designer ball gowns, blouses, slacks, dresses, shoes, coats, belts, and scarves. There were a few boxes in the far back labeled CD's and one large box labeled Vinyl's. Her closet was a high-end boutique. Dad had a smaller closet, but he had some nice things, too. Mom wasn't going to step out with a husband that wasn't properly dressed. A tux, dress shoes, designer shirts, slacks, belts. To imagine my dad wearing any of these clothes now was nearly impossible. I was so used to the overgrown scruffy beard, holey Tommy Bahama t-shirt, and wrinkly khaki shorts. A vague image of him in classy clothes formed faintly for a moment and then faded away. He also had a box of CD's. I wonder why they weren't with the other CD's in Mom's closet. Seemed kind of weird that they would separate out their CD's after 20 years of marriage.

I could sell this stuff. I know I could. People want to live like the rich even if they couldn't afford it. If I can sell this stuff at a huge discount, I can generate some cash. But how?

Chapter Twenty-five

It takes approximately 116 hours to become an internet sensation if you do something really gross.... like empty a butt load of roaches onto a middle school cafeteria table from your disgusting lunch box.

When I got on the bus the next Monday, every kid tried to show me how many views various viral videos of me were getting. One kid said, "Look, this video got 300,000 views!"

I ignored them and stared out the window, expressionless, like I had gone mute. They seemed put off that I wasn't impressed or interested. Really? Like I would be happy about this?

I knew this day was going to be hard.

I decided to take refuge in the media center before school (stay out of the courtyard where vultures circulate for carnage) and at lunch (stay out of the infamous cafeteria-the scene of the crime) and of course during study hall, where I planned on researching how to sell stuff online. We weren't supposed to use the computers for personal use, but who cares at this point.

Anticipating study hall is what would help me get through the day.

Chapter Twenty-six

I was verbally abused all day, but I kept my mind on my quest.

I had taken extensive notes on how to start an online business at lunch and when I got to study hall, I was determined to set up my virtual store.

I decided to use eBay instead of Amazon because the monthly fee was lower, only $4.95 a month, but when I tried to set up an account, there was one problem: eBay required a credit card on file. So did Amazon.

I researched how to get a credit card. My heart sank. You had to be 18 years old, even with a co-signer, to get a credit card. I had to think of some way to sell my items. It was the only way to make some money.

***

When I got off the bus that day, I waved to Winston and walked home as usual. But when I got to my driveway, my heart started beating fiercely. A mail truck was parked there.

"Do you live here?" the mailwoman asked.

Hesitantly I replied, "Yes."

"Why aren't you getting your mail out of the box?" She sounded irritated.

"I'm sorry," I stammered to come up with a lie. "My mom's been really sick." Was all I could think to say. Her face softened and became sympathetic. I realized she thought my mom might have a serious illness like cancer. I didn't correct her.

"Well, here it is. There is too much to fill the mailbox." She handed me a large box of mail, and I apologized again.

Then I blurted out, "How do I mail a package? Do I have to go to the post office?"

"No, I have some boxes right here. You can put whatever you want in these, and you are charged for the box when you ship something. Here take a few."

She grabbed several sizes for me to choose. "You mean the boxes are free?" I couldn't believe my good fortune.

"Well, yes, until you ship something. Then you pay. The price is on the box."

"Then do I take it to the post office?" I clarified.

"I can conduct the transaction if you want. I usually come by around 3pm. I was a little late today."

"Thanks." I took some flattened boxes from her just in case I figured out a way to sell my parents' stuff online and tucked them under my arm.

I waved and carried the box of mail and empty boxes to the front door and set them down. When I knew she was out of sight, I walked around back and scaled the iron gate. I went back to the front door to retrieve the box of mail and leaned the empty boxes against the wall inside the front door. Too overwhelmed to go through the mail, I set it on dad's sofa. I'll do that later.

***

The jokes and insults waned over the next two days, and no one called me Country Club Girl anymore.

Roach Girl was my name now, as if Country Club Girl never existed. And the way they said it was like it had been my name throughout all of middle school. "Hey, Roach Girl," people would say casually as they passed me, not laughing or smiling. Just a normal salutation.

They can have Country Club Girl. It wasn't me anymore. I identified more with Roach Girl. The stupid middle schoolers of Beachside think they are insulting me, but in my mind, Roach Girl was my superhero. Student by day. Conqueror of roaches, heat, silence, darkness, and loneliness by night. Roach Girl was powerful in a way Country Club Girl never was. Country Club Girl worried about straight hair, perfect makeup, the right clothes, the right friends, the right boy, the right lunch box. How trivial and stupid was that? How weak.

Roach Girl was a survivor. She endured cosmic explosions, the world turning to ice, people stomping on her. Roach Girl could do things no one she knew could do, and she was about to do more than she ever imagined was possible.

Chapter Twenty-seven

When researching what I needed for my store, I realized something that I knew, but had totally not thought of since my parents abandoned me. I could take my laptop computer to Starbucks and use their electricity and Wi-Fi. Starbucks was just a mile away and across the road from the Target shopping plaza.

I wanted to do more research. Tomorrow was the last day of school, and I would get my $100 gift card. I wanted to see if I could figure out a way to launch my business without a credit card. I needed money to survive the summer. In the back of my mind, I desperately hoped at least one parent would be home by then. If one of them did come back, I could share my plan and we could do this together. We could be partners and make a plan to get out of this mess.

If one of them were to return, which one would I want? My first thought was dad. Dad was nicer. But Mom got crap done. Dad was nicer, but nonproductive. He hadn't demonstrated the determination needed to get a big task done. Quite the opposite, really. Mom had turned into a witch, but she was functional. It was a tossup. At this point, I wouldn't care which one came home.

***

I carefully packed my laptop in my backpack and headed out on mom's bike. Once at Starbucks, I set up at a table and plugged in my computer. There was an old man with a thick book that looked like the bible open in front of him with passages highlighted. He was intensely reading it and making notes in the margins. Mom went through a bible phase during our poverty-stricken predicament. Dad refused to go, but she made me. She bought us both a study bible and we sat listening to the preacher talk about how God makes you go through difficulties in order to bring you closer to Him. How the meek shall inherit the earth. How Jesus loves you no matter what you have done. How God will bless you if only you believe. Mom eventually gave up on God. He wasn't working fast enough for her. I glanced at the man as I turned on my computer. I wonder if he was suffering. I wonder if he will give up if God doesn't fulfill his needs fast enough.

There was another table filled with women my mom's age, sipping coffee and gossiping.

I felt I needed to order something since I was using their establishment like an office. I hadn't been to a Starbucks in so long. I used to come here all the time with mom before 'the incident'. Afterwards, we would come once a week for a little treat. Eventually, we stopped coming.

I scanned the menu and was in total shock at the prices. I never gave any thought to the cost of a latte when mom brought me here. She just paid, and I would grab my Frappuccino at the end of the counter. $5.95 for one drink!! I could buy a four pack of chicken soup. That would be four nights of dinner. I looked harder and saw where a simple black coffee was about the cheapest thing they had, so I ordered a decaf. I reminded myself that I was using their Wi-Fi and setting up a business here, so I could pay for a coffee.

Now, I wanted to research how much some of mom and dad's stuff would sell for. I began looking at what people were asking for similar items. Clothes ranged in price from almost nothing to extremely expensive. I needed to find out what exactly mom and dad had as far as clothes – designer names and styles.

I didn't want to sell mom and dad's vinyls, but I was curious what people would pay for them. Wow! I couldn't believe it. Some of these went for thousands of dollars. I wrote down titles of the most expensive records and would check the box when I got home. I needed to inventory them to see what kind of gold mine I had. The vinyls would be my last resort. Hopefully, mom or dad would be home before I had to sell them.

I was done with my coffee and had a plan to start an inventory list of items. I would come back and write down how much each item was worth after school was over. Then I needed to figure out a way to sell them and get the cash.

***

Tomorrow was the last day of school and the end of year pool party at Surf's Up. It was the last place I wanted to be, but I could do it. I would just take a book and sit on a chair away from everyone.

Chapter Twenty-eight

The next morning, I woke in horror. I knew before I reached down between my legs. My period. I was so overwhelmed and preoccupied that I completely forgot about it. I remember thinking once that it was late but then just forgot. Sometimes, I would go a few months without having it at all, and mom told me that was normal for my age. I planned to ask the nurse for some pads so I didn't have to buy them, but forgot that, too.

I sat up and looked at the blood- soaked sheets. My pajama shorts were drenched, and when I stood up, a gush of blood ran down my legs. I had never had a period this bad. It was as if two months' worth of blood built up and was now gushing out of me.

I had no water to rinse off and no pads to soak up the flow.

The sun was already up and if I went to take my garden hose shower, someone might see me. I ran to the bathroom and grabbed a roll of toilet paper. There was only a little left. I had been waiting for the clubhouse to reopen so I could steal another roll. But the clubhouse pool remodel was behind schedule. Every day when I got off the bus, I would look over and see it taped off and people working.

I scrubbed and scrubbed with a towel, but a faint blood stain still appeared on my legs. I was panicking. How was I going to go to the pool party and deal with my period? The thought of the bus ride there, kids calling me roach girl, the potential of blood leaking and kids seeing it sent me into a total freak out.

I fell to the floor of the bathroom and started to cry. I couldn't stop. Like the blood drenching my sheets, tears drenched my face. Crying turned into convulsions, and I slunk down to a fetal position on the floor, clutching my cramping stomach. How could I make it to school today? I just want to stay here. Sobbing, I began choking out screams into the empty, cavernous mansion. *"Mom, how could you do this to me? I hate you! I hate you for being so self- centered! All you cared about was money and clothes and shoes and a fancy house! You didn't really love dad! I hope you never come back! You are a social climber! You are a snob! And dad, I hate you too!*

So pathetic! You have a setback in life, and you give up?! You coward! Wanting us to take pity on you for making a mistake and losing your medical license? Wanting us to say, 'poor dad'? Wanting us to pick up the pieces while you curl up on the sofa and drink? I hate you both for leaving me here! You are both cowards and I HATE YOU! I hope you never come back!"

I sobbed until I had no more tears left and was gasping for breath. Then, I slowly sat up and leaned against the bathroom cabinet to pull myself together and think. I grabbed a clean corner of the bloody towel and blew my nose. *Think Vivian. Think. Your parents made bad choices, but you don't have to. Don't let a setback hold you back. You can be stronger than them.*

If I don't go to school, I won't get my gift card. I had money left, but only $85. 07. And I had no idea if this plan of selling clothes would work. I had no idea how long it would take before I had some cash. It could be a couple of weeks, maybe longer.

I was down to three cans of peaches, half of a jar of peanut butter, and a box of Ritz crackers. There was no way I could miss school today. I needed the $100.

My period was so heavy. Could I get to school without an accident and run to the nurse? I had no choice. I had to try. Besides, after the horrible 'roach incident' who really cared what kids said to me anymore? How could it get any worse?

I pulled out a dark pair of jeans and a clean pair of underwear. I stuffed all the remaining toilet paper into my panties. I could feel the blood already soaking up the tissue. I put a book, another pair of jeans and underwear in my backpack and even though it was over 90 degrees, I put a jacket in there too—in case I had to use it to cover my bottom.

I managed to climb the gate slowly, and make it to the bus stop, nodding hello awkwardly to Winston, convinced he could tell I was walking weirdly.

I sat up tall on the bus, clenching and hoping blood didn't leak. When the bus pulled up to the school, I pretended to rummage through my bag and let everyone leave before me. I heard some kid say, 'What's up Roach Girl. Looking for a roach to eat?' I pretended not to hear him and bent further over, hiding my face with my hair. My hair. I looked at it as I hid. In my meltdown this morning, I had forgotten to even look in the mirror. Tangled clumps hung before my eyes. And the smell. I had not showered this morning and the sweat made my hair smell musty and gross like an old, moldy garage. I didn't even brush it. I fumbled around to see if I had a brush. I didn't.

I got out my jacket. I could feel the warm wetness causing my jeans to stick to my skin. I knew this was bad. I stood and wrapped the jacket around my waist and saw the blood on the seat.

The bus driver was eyeing me now. I had no choice but to say, "I had an accident."

He reached for some Clorox wipes and handed them to me. His face was patient and he seemed to understand, either from years of driving middle school girls every day or maybe he had girls of his own. "Thanks." I quickly took out two and cleaned it up. I gave them back and he held out the trash can. I sheepishly threw away the bloody squares.

Gingerly, I climbed down the bus steps and raced to the nurse. I tried to avoid the courtyard, but Mr. Kingsley spotted me and yelled, "Hey, Vivian! You did it! Perfect attendance for three years in a row!" I turned to give him a smile and nod. "I want to put you on the morning announcements and give you the award." Oh no. The last thing I wanted was to go on the news. I pretended I didn't hear him and kept walking to the nurse.

When I got to her office, she unlocked a cabinet in her private bathroom and handed me some pads. I closed the door and took off my bloodied jeans and panties. I grabbed a bunch of paper towels, wet them in the sink, and did a quick clean up of my private area and thighs. Next, I changed into the clean panties and jeans I brought, rolled the soiled clothes into a tight ball, wrapped them in some clean paper towels, and stuffed everything at the bottom of my backpack under my book.

The nurse left the cabinet unlocked and like a true criminal, I grabbed as many pads as I could stuff in the side pouch of my backpack. I closed the cabinet, hoping she would just lock it and not notice the gaping empty shelf where stacks of pads used to be.

I was truly feeling sick and weak and when I emerged from the bathroom, I must have looked bad.

The nurse sympathetically said, "Do you want to lay down?"

I nodded yes and carefully laid on the paper covered cot, curling up in fetal position.

"You are not up for this pool party, are you?" she asked.

I shook my head no. But I couldn't have her call my mom or dad. That would start a possible chain of events I wasn't in the mood to handle.

"I am feeling OK. My parents are really busy. I can make it through the day," I managed to sit up.

"Maybe I can talk to the counselor, and you could stay back and help a teacher pack up her room for the summer. Would you prefer that?"

"That would be great." My period was suddenly having benefits.

A few minutes later, the nurse came back and said, "Mrs. Miller said she would be delighted to have some help today. She isn't going on the trip. But Mrs. Pinkerton would like to speak with you first."

I wonder why? In the three years I had been at Beachside, I didn't have much contact with the school counselors. I'm surprised she even knew who I was. Why would she want to talk?

Mr. Kingsley came by the nurse's office about then and said, "There you are. Are you sick?"

The nurse gave him a look, and he stopped asking questions.

"Hey, if you aren't up for going on the news, I can just give you the award," he disappeared and a second later was back. "Here you go." He handed me the envelope paper clipped to a paper award stating, 'Perfect Attendance.'

I wanted to hug him and tell him he was the nicest person at Beachside Middle School, but I just said, "Thanks."

"Where's Mrs. Pinkerton's office?" I asked the nurse.

She escorted me there and the counselor said, "Come in and sit, Vivian."

I fidgeted, worried she was about to ask personal questions.

"Mr. Rexford called to tell me you got into Lorenzo Williams," I suddenly remembered dropping off the application. She continued, "but the phone number you gave for your parents was disconnected. He has been trying to reach you."

I quickly said, "Oh we are changing over our phone plan. We will have a new number by this weekend."

"Ok, well, he wants us to call him today and set up your schedule for the fall and review a few things before summer starts. Are you sure you want to go to Lorenzo Williams? You know it is a technical high school."

I nodded yes.

She looked at me intensely for a moment and said, "I never thought of you for a technical student. You have an impeccable academic resume. You took several high school classes already," she shook her head and continued. "I see you as more of an ivy league candidate in a few years. Technical school is......," more head shaking and hesitation. I could tell she was trying to find a politically correct way to say something. "for kids who are not as privileged as you."

Now she was looking me square in the eye. I wanted to say, '*Oh by privileged you mean pretty white Country Club girl with a doctor daddy and glamourous mommy. Well, I have news for you, Mrs. Pinkerton. Mommy, daddy, and Country Club girl have left the building.*'

She filled the silence with, "You realize you will be a minority there? You will probably be one of the only white kids. Have you been to the school?" She was sort of stammering now, realizing she was sounding racist. "I mean, it is a beautiful school. It was rebuilt a couple of years ago and is state of the art, but it is in a questionable part of town—very far from here. Your parents are OK with this decision?"

"Yes, Mrs. Pinkerton. My parents are fine with it." To get her off my back and lose suspicion, I made up a little lie and said, "I love architecture. I have been fascinated with it my whole life. By going to the tech school, I will have a unique resume and have a better chance at getting into a prestigious architectural school."

This seemed to satisfy her, and she slowly nodded. "I could see this as an advantage. Different, but you are right. Colleges look for different. Then she picked up the phone and began dialing.

"Hi Mr. Rexford. This is Bev at Beachside. I have Vivian here with me now," she punched the speaker button.

"Congratulations, Vivian! You are a new Lorenzo Williams Mustang!"

I smiled a little. He had such a happy voice.

"I want to go over a few things with you, OK?"

"Ok," I replied.

"First, do you have a phone number? We tried the ones you gave on your application, but they didn't work," he sounded so kind, like not having a valid phone number was no big deal to him.

"We are switching plans. I'll have one by the weekend," I stated, thinking I would solve that problem later.

"Ok, call us Monday with that information. Our office is open all summer."

Mrs. Pinkerton piped in, "I'll give her your number."

"Great! Ok. A few things I want to go over. We are a Title I school and what that means is that 73% of our students are from poverty- stricken families, therefore, we provide a free breakfast and lunch to all students. Now, I know you won't need that service, but it is provided for you anyway. The first day of school is August 12th and your bus number is 333. The bus will pick you up in front of the guard house of your development at 5:50am each morning so you need to be there 10 minutes prior to that. I know that is early, Vivian, but you live on the north side of town and that is quite a distance from the school. You are the only person riding that bus."

I loved the sound of that.

He continued, "Let's go over your schedule. You took four high school classes this year and that is great. You will be able to get into your programs earlier than most, probably your sophomore year instead of your junior year."

I interrupted, "What do you mean? I am not going to take carpentry next year?" My voice sounded disappointed, but I couldn't help it. I wanted to fix my house--*now*.

He chuckled, "You will need to take your basic high school classes to get them out of the way. Then you can take the trade skills. I have you set to take Honors Geometry, Honors English, Honors Biology, Spanish II, Honors History, and I can probably get you into the introductory drafting class since you have so many high school credits already."

"What is the drafting?" I asked.

"Sort of like a basic architecture class. Designing buildings."

"Ok," I said.

"Do you have any more questions?" He asked.

I couldn't think of any. I was thinking about getting free breakfast and lunch which would cut down on my grocery needs and how I was hoping to learn the trades immediately.

"Don't forget. Call us Monday with your phone number. And welcome, Vivian. Have a great summer, and I'll see you in August."

Chapter Twenty-nine

"Hi, Vivian. You are just what I need today. And don't forget your King Henry VIII project. You left it here yesterday. It was quite spectacular. One of the best posters and information I have ever gotten. You are such a talented artist."

She paused as she handed me my poster, "Is everything OK?" She was studying me hard. I knew I looked like crap and tried to neaten my wild hair with my hands before taking the poster from her. "Yea."

"Are you sure?" She looked down at my poster and continued. "I noticed you added a small roach crawling out of the basket here." She pointed to the roach which I suddenly realized I had drawn and colored with great detail. The bloody head was hanging in mid-air about to land in the intricately drawn mud-colored basket. I didn't think anyone would really notice the tiny roach, but now looking at it, the tiny roach was such a drastic contrast to the enormous bloody head that it really stood out.

"I know about the roach incident in the cafeteria. I know the kids call you Roach Girl now, and you no longer sit with your friends in class. I also know that you decided to go to Lorenzo Williams. Are you sure you want to go there, Vivian? You don't really seem like the type of kid who goes to a technical school."

Again? Another person making this comment.

I couldn't help myself and said, "What type of kid goes there?" My tone sounded defensive.

"Well, most kids that go to Lorenzo are interested in trade skills. You are a straight A student taking all advanced classes and even high school classes. Gulfside High is for students like you. College bound. Lorenzo is for kids who are better suited for labor type jobs. It just doesn't seem like you, and I want to make sure you aren't making this decision because of anything going on with your friends or at home."

I was getting good at thinking fast. "Well, we have had a roach problem, and my mom hates chemicals, so she has been trying this homemade herbal concoction that my dad says is just attracting more roaches. After what happened at school, I told her, and she called the exterminator. That problem is fixed. And Mr. Rexford said many of his students go to college." This was a lie. I had no idea and Mr. Rexford never said that, but it seems like if they wanted to go to college, they could.

"Ok, just don't make a quick decision because you had a falling out with your friends. Those things will pass," she smiled and meant well, but she didn't understand. I was Roach Girl to all of them and that would carry over to high school. I knew it would. Brianna wanted to be queen. She wanted Langston to be her king. And I am sure she wants to rule high school, so she will keep the 'Roach Girl' alive to make sure I don't regain Country Club Girl status. Little did Brianna know that I hated Country Club Girl now and had no desire to be her again.

I wanted a skill. I wanted to work. I needed money now. I couldn't care less about who was popular or even going to college. What if I didn't want to go to college? How could I afford college anyway?

I could tell she was still skeptical. "I really want to be a builder one day or an architect. I can learn all the trades and that will help me."

"Hmmm. You never struck me as a construction kind of girl, but an architect I can see. You have a gift for creative design. I can see that from the poster you drew."

We were both looking at the poster. I broke the silence and changed the subject.

"Think about all those queens. How scared they all must have been, living with a madman of a King, at his mercy, worried they would be the next one out of favor, wondering if they would get the chopping block or hopefully, exiled to a distant castle, cast aside and their fate determined by a force out of their control. Everyone thinks that being a princess or queen would be grand, but in reality, being the poor, country girl, able to marry the man you love or freely live without the watchful eye of a kingdom, is the true treasure. That is real freedom. Don't you think?"

She smiled then and said, "I agree. You are a wise young girl."

I helped her all morning, organizing shelves and packing boxes.

When the day was over, she hugged me and said good luck at Lorenzo.

Chapter Thirty

That afternoon when I got off the bus, I did feel somewhat free. Free of school at least.

Winston waved and said, "The pool and clubhouse are back open. You can restart your swim training."

I smiled. What started out as a disastrous day of bloodshed, actually turned out OK. School was over, and I wouldn't have to face anyone from Beachside Middle School ever again because I was now a student at Lorenzo Williams Technical High School. I had a backpack full of pads and wouldn't need to buy any for at least two or three months, I could once again shower and gather water at the clubhouse and didn't need to use the garden hose anymore nor would I have to poop like an animal behind a bush, and I had my gift card in my hand to buy some groceries.

I also had my business idea to make some money over the summer and was in control of my own fate. Suddenly, I felt liberated, powerful, and ready to take charge of my own destiny.

I scaled the iron gate with Olympic agility, forgetting I had my period and a huge pad lodged in my pants, and then stopped abruptly when I stood back up.

My hidden entrance door was wide open.

Chapter Thirty-one

My heart was beating wildly. I had grown so used to my routine of entering the taped- up French door, that I no longer worried about leaving the door unlocked every day. Did I accidentally leave it open when I left this morning? I *was* overly concerned about jumping the iron gate with my period being so bad and only having a few tissues wedged in my panties. But I remember looking at my reflection in the window of the closed door because I was going so slow over the gate, thinking to myself 'Is this my life now? Creeping around hoping no one will discover my secret?' Yes, I definitely remember the door being closed.

Someone was in my house or had been in my house. Should I go in? What choice did I have? I couldn't exactly go tell Winston. He would find out what was going on and report me to someone who would take me away to live with strangers. No. I had to go inside.

I carefully tiptoed into the house, so silent, no one would be able to hear me. Listening intently for any creek or shuffle or breath, I started in mom's room looking under her bed, in her closet, in dad's closet, and in their bathroom. Empty.

Next, I checked my room and closet. Nothing. What would I do if I found someone? Attack? Run? I did a quick mental check of my exit route if needed. My bathroom was empty, too. The rest of the house was easier to check out because of the lack of dry wall covering the framing.

I still crept quietly into each room to see who might be lurking.

In one of the extra bedrooms, there were six giant boxes that said 'wardrobe' on them. These boxes had been here ever since we moved in, but they were so big and bulky that I suddenly realized they could house a person. Was my mind making me crazy? I decided to check out the rest of the house and then come back and check out these boxes just in case.

When I got to the kitchen, in the corner, I saw the intruder. A raccoon. My heart leapt at first with fear and then released into relief. He looked like he was lost and probably disappointed. Raccoons love food and I didn't have much, except for a couple of cans of fruit and soup and a jar of peanut butter. I opened the door to the patio, and he scurried out by the pool. I followed him and opened the screen door to let him free. I doubt he would come looking for food here again.

I thought to myself, I need to buy a new lock for that door. Next time, it might not be a raccoon that gets in. The rational part of my brain knew that the door was opened by the masked critter, but when you live alone and don't have another person to tell you you are being irrational, your mind can be a galaxy of gross exaggeration. Those giant wardrobe boxes were now obsessing me. I was imagining a person hiding in one, waiting until dark to creep into my room and attack, or worse, several people, one in each of the boxes ready to ambush me in the middle of the night.

Feeling compelled to release these images from my brain, I grabbed a knife and crept back to the room housing the fictitious felons. I cut the tape off the first box which was almost as tall as me. These boxes were different from a normal box. The lid had a foldable top that I had to lift over and lay on the back of the box, exposing a bar with clothes hung tightly crammed together. It was like a box closet.

At first, I thought, good more clothes for me to sell. Then I noticed something that made me tingle with excitement. All of these clothes had tags on them. I ran my hand along the sleeves of blouses and jackets, grabbing occasional tags and reading prices that shocked me.

I quickly opened the other boxes. More clothes with tags. Each of the six boxes were packed tightly with store bought clothes that had not only never been worn, but still had tags to prove it. I felt like a miner that had just struck gold.

As I looked closely at the designer clothes and their tags, my excitement morphed into fury. What was mom's problem? Why would she buy this stuff and not even wear it? She had to have purchased all of it before 'the incident' because the clothes were in storage boxes and had been there a long time. She wouldn't spend this kind of cash when dad was out of work, and we could hardly pay bills. Or would she? Maybe she had a shopping sickness and couldn't fit anything else in her closet and bought these boxes to store stuff. Regardless, who spends mountains of money on clothes?

Stupid people. Selfish people. People who leave you because you are poor. People with no heart or soul. People who should go to the chopping block for being so narcissistic. And why would she leave without taking any of these things she just 'had to buy' with her?

I remember the morning I found the note taped to the mirror. I vaguely heard her leaving with her suitcase, quietly rolling down the concrete hallway. She took just what fit in that case. Was she planning on returning for everything else?

If she was, she was going to have the shock of her life because I was planning on selling every stinking thing that represented her. I was going to wipe her materialistic self out of my existence.

My summer sweatshop was about to open for business.

Chapter Thirty-two

After an early morning swim in the newly renovated clubhouse pool, I showered and got dressed.

The locker room door that led into the clubhouse restaurant opened and a woman entered. "Hi, nice to have the pool back, isn't it? And the locker room looks great, doesn't it?"

"Yea," I said as little as possible.

"Hey, I think I may have something that is yours. Stay right there." She left and came back a couple of minutes later.

In one hand, she had the bathing suit I left in a locker before the renovation. In the other hand, she had a giant muffin. "The construction crew emptied out the lockers before they demoed the place. I remember seeing you up here each morning wearing this," she handed me the suit. "And I was wondering if you wanted one of my soon-to-be famous muffins. I am trying a new recipe that is gluten free and want your honest opinion."

I was ravenous from the swim and hadn't had a muffin in so long, I couldn't even remember. My diet consisted of cold canned soup, canned fruit, peanut butter sandwiches and crackers, and water from the garden hose. I felt my mouth salivate.

I took the muffin and tried not to look like a starved street kid. "Hmmm. Really good."

And it was. I resisted the temptation to lick the crumbs from the wrapper that had housed this delicious bundle of decadence. How could something this simple bring me so much joy? Before 'the incident' I probably wouldn't have given any thought if someone offered me a muffin. Probably would have said no or not liked it because it was gluten free and thrown it away.

But right this minute I realized how hungry I was. Hungry to eat normal again. Hungry to not constantly feel ache in my stomach. I thought, '*maybe once I start making money, I'll treat myself to muffins.*'

"Wait here." She ran out again and came back with a cold glass of milk.

I drank it down in one long continuous gulp, realizing I must look like that starved street kid.

She just smiled, and I thanked her.

Roach Girl origin trilogy one

Chapter Thirty-three

When I returned home, I went out to the concrete living room and flopped down on dad's ratty sofa next to the large box of mail I still hadn't touched. The faint smell of stale wine wafted in the air. I had to think of a way to sell all this stuff. I knew I was sitting on a gold mine. I knew it was going to be my only way to survive alone.

I was too young to get a job and too young for a credit card to open an eBay or Amazon account. So, starting an online business was not an option.

Think.

I stared at the post office boxes leaning against the wall by the front door, and then my eyes drifted to mom's bike next to the boxes.

Mom's bike.

Dad's bike……..the Priceless Pawn…..Mom got $450 for dad's bike at the Priceless Pawn.

Selling mom's bike was out of the question. It was my only transportation…. but maybe the Priceless Pawn would buy some other things.

My mind wheeled with what to do next. Find out where the Priceless Pawn was located. Find out how I would get there. Find what items to sell first.

I jumped up and went to Mom's closet and found the most elaborate ball gown I could find. A Valentino long sleeved floral embroidered silk organza evening gown with a jewel neckline, strapless allusion, A-line silhouette, and floor sweeping hem. The dress was a piece of art. I scrutinized the purses aligned on one shelf and found a Saint Laurent clutch beaded handbag. Next, shoes. Mom had rows and rows of shoes. I settled on elegant Gucci black heels. I gently laid the ensemble on Mom's bed.

Next, I went to Dad's closet and pulled out a box in the far corner labeled 'vinyls.' I peeled off the packing tape and opened the box. On top was a Bob Dylan album titled: "Blood on the Tracks." It was encased in plastic, and I set it beside Mom's gown.

I grabbed a piece of paper and pencil from my nightstand and wrote down the album title and the designer label of the gown, shoes, and handbag. I shoved it into my backpack along with my wallet and computer and hopped on Mom's bike.

***

Once at Starbucks, I logged onto the Wi-Fi and found where the Priceless Pawn was located. I would have to take the city bus because it was all the way on the south side of town. There was no way I could bike that far carrying items to sell. I looked up city bus schedules and pick-up locations. There was a bus stop right in front of the Target Plaza. The next time for pick-up was 1:00pm. It was 10am now, so I could easily make it.

Then I looked up how much the Bob Dylan album was worth. Sealed, it is listed for $150. Finding the ball gown took more searching, but eventually I found the exact gown listed for $8,500! I could not believe my mom would pay that much money for a dress! What was wrong with her? She only wore it once, that I can remember. The shoes were listed for $800, and the handbag was $2,100!

My excitement and anticipation of how much money I could possibly get by the end of the day if I sold these things, was suddenly replaced with pure anger and hatred. How could my mom spend so much money on one outfit that she only wore once? She always made it seem like dad was the cause of our problems, but now I wondered if that was really true. Back when dad used to fight with mom, I remembered him saying how much pressure she put on him to make money. I see it now. How could any human keep up with someone who had to spend this kind of money on a dress? I wanted to pick up the computer and hurl it against the wall. I wanted to shout at the top of my lungs.

But I didn't.

Instead, I sat in shock as Langston and Brianna walked through the door holding hands.

Flustered, I began packing up my computer. I got what I needed and what I didn't need was a fake conversation with them. I know they saw me, but I pretended I didn't see them. I zipped up my backpack and whisked right by them without saying a word.

My heart slowed down once I was out the door. I stopped at Target and locked my bike with a large lock I had found in the garage. It had never been used, and the padlock still had the key in it. I tucked the key in a side pocket of my backpack and raced into the store. I picked up a new lock and handle for the back French door and a few grocery items.

Back at the house, I rummaged through Dad's tools and set out to complete my first construction project: replace the broken lock and handle. I fumbled through the directions and finally figured it out. The satisfaction of fixing the door handle on my own was incredibly fulfilling. I knew it was a small accomplishment, but I imagined myself fixing everything in this house and how good it would make me feel.

Next, I found some packing tape and carefully assembled one of the boxes the mail woman gave me. Then, I placed the shoes and handbag on the bottom, carefully folded the gown, placing it on top of the shoes and bag, and finally set the Bob Dylan album on top. I taped up the box. I took my computer out of my backpack and made sure I had my wallet with some cash for the bus and a water canteen. I locked the French door behind me and put the new key carefully in a tiny, zippered flap inside my backpack.

I decided not to ride my bike to the bus stop. It wasn't far at all and even though I noticed there was a bike rack next to the bus stop bench on the ride back from Target, I didn't trust leaving Mom's expensive bike there all day. I had no idea how long this adventure would last.

By 12:50, I was sitting on a bench waiting for the bus. For a moment, I wondered what would happen if Langston or Brianna or any of the gang saw me sitting here. But the bus wheezed to an abrupt stop in front of me, and as I stood, I realized I didn't care.

At 1:00, I was sitting on a bus heading to the Priceless Pawn.

Chapter Thirty-four

I remember when mom and I were riding with the police officer to the Priceless Pawn. I remember being confused and alarmed at how she was acting. Her overly flirtatious lies led me to lose a little respect for her that day and left me feeling lost and lonely sitting in the back seat of that police car. Why was she lying? Who cares what a police officer thinks. She did. Her phony façade wasn't fooling me. A frightening feeling had flooded my body in the back seat of that car that day. We were in trouble. Big trouble. Trouble that led to lies. Trouble that led to leaving.

As the bus bounced smoothly away from the north side of town, the buildings changed. New ones were replaced with older, run down ones. Some had bars on the windows. Some had weeds sprouting high between the cracks of broken concrete sidewalks and driveways. Some looked vacant. Others held sketchy businesses. 'Lone Sharks.' 'Louie's Liquor.' 'Penny Market.' 'Girls, Girls, Girls.'

This neighborhood scared me, like it did when I came here with mom in that police car. Buildings with barred windows, people in raggedy clothes roaming up and down the street – some stopped at the corner just talking and smoking- others lumbering aimlessly. One lady just standing on the sidewalk chanting something unrecognizable. Afraid? Why? I, too, was living like a bum. I defecated in bushes. I took garden hose showers in someone else's yard. Why should I be afraid? Maybe these people once lived in a mansion? Maybe they once had a great job? Or a family? I was living just like them but hidden from view. I was protected by a brick fortress with a guard at the entrance, but I rummaged in the trash for roach infested bread. How was I any different?

As the bus pulled up to a bench in front of the Priceless Pawn, I was afraid to depart. Come on Roach Girl. Get tougher. You can't be squashed. You can do this. You are a survivor – just like these people.

I stood with my box and asked the driver when the bus was going back to the north side Target. He said 6:00pm. I had no way of telling time. I didn't own a watch. I had no phone. I had been using the battery-operated CD player at home.

"What time is it now?" I asked.

"2:00," he replied.

I exited and walked swiftly into the Priceless Pawn.

Once inside, I didn't waste time. I marched straight to the counter like my mom had done when we sold Dad's bike.

As I was opening my box, a man emerged and asked, "What do you have there?"

"A Bob Dylan album and a ball gown," I tried to sound confident.

He picked up the Dylan record and turned it over.

"I'll give you $60," he stated matter-a-fact-like.

My heart sank. "I saw them online for $150."

"Yea, but I have to make some money you know." He was studying me now. Probably thinking....... what is a young girl doing here.... hawking her daddy's stuff. Whatever he was thinking he never said. I'm sure he has heard every sad story there is. People are desperate when they enter his store. Like my mom. But mom never appeared desperate when she sold Dad's bike. She truly acted like she was doing it for me, so I could get a new phone and learn the value of money. I remember her repeating that to the pawn guy after she had said it to the police officer. It was as if coming up with the perfect lie suddenly made it true, and she believed it.

He hesitated and said, "OK, $70. I have some collectors that will like this. What else you got?" He peered into my box and looked up at me quickly. "We don't sell clothes here."

My heart sank again, and it must have shown.

"Look sweetheart," he reached under the counter and handed me a business card. "Take the clothes to Sharon Rich. She owns a consignment store for fancy folks. Her place is about eight blocks straight west, towards the beach." He was pointing across the busy road. "When you cross over the railroad tracks, it is two more blocks. Just before you get to 5th Avenue where all the ritzy stores are. She can sell that fancy dress."

I took the card. 'Sharon's Riches' was written in bold cursive writing and in smaller print was an address and phone number next to a sketch of a classy lady in fancy clothes.

When the man was retrieving my $70, I looked at the jewelry displayed in the glass counter. There were several watches.

Before he handed me my money, I asked, "How much for one of these watches?" Suddenly realizing I needed to know what time it was, so I wouldn't miss my bus back to the north side.

"I have a special on watches right now. I have a beauty here for $50."

"Does it work?"

"It is 2:15pm and that is exactly what the watch says."

"I'll give you $25."

He smirked like it was funny to see a kid confidently bargain with him.

"$30."

"OK," I said, and he handed me the watch and counted out $40.

Chapter Thirty-five

I decided that the only way to overcome my fear of this neighborhood was to walk with a determined purpose. After stuffing the $40 and Sharon Rich's business card in my wallet and putting on the watch, I shoved my wallet into my backpack and secured it on my back. Then I marched out the front door of the Priceless Pawn with the box that held Mom's ball gown, shoes, and handbag firmly under one arm.

I went straight to the corner, pushed the button to hurry up the light like I had done it a thousand times, like I was comfortable here, like this was my neighborhood. When the light finally turned, I walked quickly across the street and straight west like the pawn man told me to do.

Once past the busy intersection, the street grew quiet and a different kind of scary. The houses were tiny and would best be described as dilapidated shacks. Some owners attempted to fix up their dwelling by painting their little house a wild color like mint green or pink or orange. Mom would have called these places dumps and scurried out of this neighborhood as fast as she could. Funny thing about it, Mom couldn't even afford to buy one of these places, yet she would die if she had to live here.

By the third block of tiny shanties, I was breathing better. No one had run out to kidnap me, and I saw the railroad tracks ahead like the pawn man said. I could even see giant palm trees and nicer-looking buildings in the near distance. When I got to the tracks, I looked both ways, however, I didn't think a train had run on these tracks for decades. The tracks were rusty and dry. After crossing them, the landscape changed dramatically. The businesses were posh, and I recognized the area. Mom and I took a cooking class together at a fancy kitchen store near here. I remember the candle shop on the corner.

Just like the pawn man said, Sharon's Riches was two blocks past the tracks. I entered carefully and was immediately struck by how cool the place was. Cool as in interesting. If King Henry VIII opened a shop with a hippy from the 60's, this would be it. Two giant plush purple velvet chairs sat side by side with an ornate gold accent table separating them. Concrete slate flooring was a contrasting texture to the enormous faux zebra skinned rug under the chairs and table. Clothes were displayed on various platforms throughout the space. Full body mirrors with intricate gold framing leaned strategically against the walls. And the crystal chandelier gave the place a modern castle feel. Funky music played softly, and the air smelled like cool fresh limes and ginger. It was hard to believe that the clothes were second hand. Everything looked new. I had never been in a store like it and wondered why Mom had never brought me here.

A lady came out from the back that must have been the owner, Sharon. Aside from my mom, this woman was one of the prettiest ladies I'd ever met. She was tall and had long straight black hair. Her skin was milky white, and her eyes were large and dark brown like espresso coffee. Her make-up was beautifully done, and her outfit was eclectic and chic. She flashed a dazzling smile.

"What can I do for you?" Her voice seemed kind and her eyes sparkled with a welcoming warmth.

"I have a dress, shoes, and handbag I was wondering if you would buy from me." I set the box on a beautiful table and opened it. I pulled out the breathtaking gown. Sharon let out a tiny gasp of approval. "I brought shoes and a handbag to match." Another ohhh of delight.

"These are exquisite," she said. She looked at me closer, checking me out. I felt uncomfortable all of the sudden. "Is this your dress?" she asked skeptically.

"No, it is my mom's." I was prepared for this. I figured the pawn guy would want to know if I had permission to sell such fancy stuff, so I had prepared a fabricated half-truth. "My mother died of cancer a year ago and all her clothes have been untouched in her closet ever since. My dad is too heartbroken to look at them, and we are hard up for money with all the medical bills from her fight with cancer. He told me to see if we could get some money for them. My dad is too heartbroken to do it himself, and I know he is also embarrassed because we once were rich and now, we can hardly pay our bills."

She looked about to cry. "Let me look up the gown on my price check program. I'll do the same for the shoes and bag." I suddenly felt bad for lying to her. But what choice did I have? I had to get some money and my mom *was* gone and my dad *was* heartbroken. And we were once rich and now could hardly pay our bills.

She came back after a few minutes and said, "Well, these are some pricey items, but you knew that, right? What I do is take things in on consignment. That means I display your items and when they sell, you get your money and I take a cut for selling it for you. Sometimes I buy items outright, but this gown is worth so much. I don't have that kind of cash laying around. It is sort of like we are business partners. I know what your mom probably paid for the gown, but I have no idea what someone else will pay for it. It is truly one of a kind, and I have some very wealthy clients that look for unique treasures like this. I just don't know how much someone will pay for it."

I wasn't sure how to feel. I was disappointed that I wasn't going to walk out of here with some cash, but I liked the idea of being partners with Sharon. A newfound energy surged through my body and coursed through my veins. This could be the answer to my problems. I tingled with excitement.

"OK," I said. "Let's be partners."

"Great! I will need some information from you," she walked around the table and grabbed a form and a pen.

Uh oh.

"I need your address and phone number."

I gave her my address. I really didn't think there was harm in that. I lived on the other side of town and in a rich neighborhood. If she looked me up, my story would appear real. She couldn't get past the guard, nor would she have a reason to, so I was OK with her knowing my address. The phone number was a bigger problem.

"I don't have a phone right now. We are changing phone plans, but I will soon."

"Well, I need to be able to reach you if the clothes sell."

I suddenly had a brilliant idea. "Do you need help in the store? I could come in a couple of times a week to clean and arrange clothes, and I have so many clothes to bring to you. I could stock this place for a year."

She was thinking hard, staring at the magnificent gown she had already put on a velvet bodice mannequin ready to showcase in the bay window. I repeated, "*You have no idea* how many clothes I can bring you for your store."

She agreed to let me come in on Fridays and Saturdays to start. She said those were her busiest days of the week and she always needed help organizing new inventory on those days. She never asked my age or told me how much she would pay me – if anything. She just said that the store opened at 10am.

I left Sharon's Riches so excited that I didn't realize I turned the wrong way. I had gone a block south by accident and turned down an alley to get back to the road I was on, but the alley curved and when I got to the next street, I didn't recognize anything.

I saw the railroad tracks and knew I needed to head that way to get back to the Priceless Pawn and the bus stop, so I crossed them. But now I was on a different street and didn't recognize the new batch of shacks. And the further I walked into shantytown, the more I didn't recognize.

Uh oh. I was lost.

Chapter Thirty-six

I looked at my new used watch. 3:33pm. I had plenty of time to get to the bus stop by six. In fact, I didn't know what I was going to do when I got there and that made me nervous, too. I just kept walking east and figured I would come to the busy street that the Priceless Pawn was on sooner or later.

I walked faster and faster.

I could see a busy road ahead, and then I heard a loud roaring noise above me. I looked up and a jet was descending overhead, looking like it was going to land on the next street over.

When I finally made it to the busy road, I realized I was next to the airport. I looked hard the other way and saw the Priceless Pawn in the distance. Whew. I knew where I was.

Since I had a ton of time to kill, I decided to walk over to the airport and watch some planes land. The airport was small and there were rows of jets parked around the runways. I sat on a picnic bench right outside of the small terminal.

Another jet was waiting near the terminal with the stairs down. Either someone was getting off soon or someone was getting on.

A person in a black and white uniform emerged from the jet, walked down the steps and over to the terminal door. He opened it, and a man and woman walked out. The uniformed man grabbed the elegant couple's bags and followed them to the jet.

Then my spine stiffened, and I stood. I ran to the chain link fence and clutched a gray metal link. The woman. Her hair. Long, thick, blonde. Movie star hair. I heard her laugh. Did I recognize that laugh? I hadn't heard it in so long I wasn't sure. No. It couldn't be. Turn lady. Turn. It can't be you.

The beautiful blonde turned just enough for me to glimpse her gorgeous profile before she disappeared into the jet.

Mom.

Chapter Thirty-seven

I staggered back to the picnic table and sat, bewildered, my heart pumping so fast I thought it would burst from my chest. I didn't know whether to start screaming, crying, or running. I blinked a few times staring at the jet that had yet to take off. Did I dream what I just saw? Why wasn't I screaming at her? Why wasn't I yelling *'Mom! It's me! Where are you going? Come home?'* I think a part of me didn't want to believe it was her. Laughing. Having fun. Not a care in the world.

Another airport worker pulled the stairs away from the jet and the uniformed man closed the door. The jet started to roll away smoothly from the terminal toward the runway. Where was she going? Who was she with? How could she be laughing? She left me. Alone. With a drunken depressed dad, unpaid bills, no food, no water,

no electricity. How could she just fly away from here....
from me?

Suddenly furious and curious, I marched into the
little terminal and up to the counter where an older man
stood.

"Can you tell me who was on that plane that just
left?" I asked.

"I'm sorry, little lady, but no. That information is
confidential." He went back to his computer monitor.

"But I think I know who was on that plane. She
is my," and I stopped abruptly. I couldn't tell this old
man I thought that was my mom. He would get nosy.
Then what? Maybe it wasn't my mom. Maybe he would
call the police. He looks like the type to call the police.
They would follow me and ask questions. Follow me
home. Demand to speak to a parent. See the empty shell
I was camping in and see I was alone. No. Don't say
another word. "Aunt. I thought that was my aunt. I was
going to say hi. But now that I think about it, it couldn't
have been her. She is in Paris. My mistake."

I turned and left. Once I was out the door, I
glanced through the smoky glass to see if the man was
looking suspiciously at me, but he was studying the
computer monitor.

I made my way back to the Priceless Pawn in a
zombie-like trance, passing a bum and some sketchy

looking people, but I was too shocked by my mother's betrayal to be scared. I sat on the bus stop bench. Alone.

I heard another roar and looked up as the jet soared above me.

My mother was sitting in a jet. In new fancy clothes. With new fancy luggage. With a new fancy man. Laughing. Flying far away from here.

Chapter Thirty-eight

I pressed my forehead against the city bus window on the way back to the north side of Portofino, watching the bar-windowed businesses roll past me. Priceless Pawn. Couples Cavern. Dan's Auto. Spanish Market. As the bus picked up speed, the businesses blurred until the bus rolled to an abrupt stop again. I recognized the Northside Hospital with royal palm trees lining the entrance. I was born in that hospital. Suddenly, the streets were cleaner, newer, nicer.

I thought back to my walk from the Priceless Pawn to Sharon's Riches and how crossing the railroad tracks literally divided two completely different worlds. A person could easily walk across the tracks from one world to another, but people rarely did. As if the tracks were a barrier that might as well be a 50-foot concrete unscalable wall. And if you dare to cross over, you will trip and crack your head on the steal rail, leaving blood on the tracks.

People were afraid of the side of the tracks with the shacks. As if being poor made you a scary person, with a house full of roaches, water and electricity that got cut off because you couldn't pay your bills, drunk, out-of-work dads passed out on sofas, mothers who prostitute themselves to get by, criminals who hawk other peoples' things at the Priceless Pawn to pay the rent.

Were they afraid that the poor people would hurt them? Or were they afraid to face the possibility that they might have to live in a shack if something went wrong in their world? Were they afraid if they accidentally drove into that neighborhood, they would face a reality they didn't want to face.

I didn't want to go back to the south side of town again. I wanted to pretend I never saw mom getting on that jet. I wanted to live in the fantasy that she was going to come back soon.

But why would she now? Leave that luxury life to live with a loser who gave up living? *But what about me? Didn't she want me?* I can see why she left dad. I was furious with him, too. Didn't she beg him for years to move on? Didn't she want it to work? He drove her away. *But why wouldn't she take me?* Why would she leave me to deal with dad when *she* couldn't even do it? How can a 13-year-old do what she couldn't even do?

Maybe that wasn't really her. I was so desperate that I imagined it was her…. maybe…. but that laugh…. that hair…..

I felt queasy. All I had eaten was that muffin this morning. My mouth felt like cotton. My head felt dizzy. I reached for my water bottle and took a few sips, then a few more. I felt better. Laying my head back against the seat, I stopped looking out the window and closed my eyes.

Sharon said I could help her on Fridays and Saturdays. I was so excited. *Was*. But now I didn't want to go. I wanted to curl up on my bed and never wake up. At that moment, I understood dad. Life was overwhelming. Why even try? Dad gave up. Maybe I should just give up, too.

As far as mom was concerned, she did die. I said it to Sharon and now it is true in my mind. Just like when mom told the lie about Dad's bike to the policeman and then the pawn man. She was so convincing. Like saying it suddenly made it true in her mind. That is how I felt about the cancer lie. Mom was dead to me.

No need to be afraid of blood on the tracks. No need to be afraid of the airport and the ghost of your dead mother. Grow up, Vivian. You're a big girl now.

G. Keller

Chapter Thirty-nine

The night was hard. I was exhausted, but the heat made it impossible to sleep. Darkness so black that if I stretched my hands at arms- length, I couldn't see them at all. I hated the dark. Roaches loved the dark. I could hear them faintly scratch as they scurried across the wall. I didn't freak if one found its way to my body. I would just reach to the back of my neck or leg or head and grab it in my palm where I would crush the critter. I used to get up and dump the remains into the trash, but now I just leaned over the side of the bed and let the severed legs and wings and what was left of the body float to the floor of my room.

What I hated most at night was the silence. The heat made me sleepless, but the silence made me think. Think *too* much. My mom used to tell me that when I was little. I would think about the starving people in

Africa or see a homeless person on the side of the road and start to cry. Mom would say, "Stop crying. You think too much." I remember being confused and hurt when she said it. Like I had some flaw—the too sensitive flaw. Now all I could think about was how pathetic my parents were to leave me. About how pathetic my friends were to leave me. About how was I going to survive alone— could I do it or not?

Fear was like a snake that slithered into your hot, dark thoughts, coiling around your brain and heart and soul until it squeezed you so hard you couldn't breathe. You had a choice. Just lay there and let it suffocate you until you die, or reach for its scaly body and struggle futilely to free yourself from its vice grip, ultimately losing against its power, or reach for a giant butcher knife and have the courage to slice it in half, letting the blood drip all over you and possibly get a poisonous, painful bite before it withers and gradually grows limp enough for you to peel out of its clenches.

You think the choice is easy when you aren't in the middle of crippling fear. Of course, you think to yourself, *I would slay the viper off my body. Who cares about a little blood? Who cares about a little bite?* But when real fear, lonely fear, hungry fear, I don't know how to go on fear finds you, it is easy to grow weary and just let it suffocate you. You see, fear doesn't find you when you feel strong enough to fight. It finds you when you are too tired, too weak, too hopeless to fight. Easy prey. That is what it looks for. Fear is a coward.

I had to think of something to fight the silence so my mind wouldn't think too much. I grabbed my flashlight and crept carefully over to Mom's room, her old room. I found her box of CDs and opened it. On top were several CDs not in cases. I never heard my mom listen to music. Ever. They were slightly dusty, but not as much as I would have thought. I guess the box protected them. She must have listened to these the most. I was suddenly sort of curious of my mom's musical taste. As I exited the closet, I remembered my dad had his own box of CDs. I ripped off the taped-up top, and he, too, had a couple of cds out of their cases. Like mom, I had never heard dad listen to music other than the car radio. I tried to think back to when I was little to remember if we ever danced to the stereo or cooked in the kitchen listening to music, but I couldn't recall an occasion.

I took dad's CDs and kept them separate from mom's. I wanted to see the difference in the music they listened to.

Back in my room, I used the hurricane supply kit CD/radio player to play the first selection. I spread out mom's and dad's CDs on the floor and flashed light across the titles. I instantly noticed something. There was a CD that both of them owned: Fleetwood Mac: Rumours. They must have each had this CD before they married. Why else would there be two of the same CD? I would start with this one. Maybe there was a secret clue in a song that would help me understand them better. Understand why they fell in love. Understand why they fell apart. Understand why they left me. Maybe once, long ago, they shared something in common. Something besides money. Maybe there was a clue that would give me hope they would come home.

I listened to all the songs with my eyes closed, hoping it would help me drift into sleep, but sweat rolling off my body and two overly friendly roaches who had found my feet, kept me awake.

I found the music interesting. Like nothing I had ever really heard before. I decided to hit the repeat button and let the music play over and over again in hopes the mellow, rhythmic sounds would win my fight against sleeplessness.

But sleeplessness won. Around the third trip through the Rumours CD, I settled on my two favorite tracks: number 2 'Dreams' and number 7 'The Chain'. I grabbed the music box and rested it next to me like a pet, with my arms curled around it. I would bypass the other songs to get to 'Dreams' and 'The Chain', soon having them memorized and singing along.

Singing made me less lonely. Less scared.

My voice sounded different each time I sang the songs – richer, fuller. No longer did my voice sound tinny and weak, evaporating when it hit the air like when I tried to remember the words to 'The Sound of Silence.'

Now my voice was filling the room like Dad's used to fill the car. I turned the stereo down so I could hear my voice better. Realizing no one could hear me, I began belting out the songs with such unbridled confidence that my defeated mood was diminishing. As my voice became stronger, I became stronger.

Dreams by Fleetwood Mac

Now   here   you   go   again
You   say   you   want   your   freedom
Well,   who   am   I   to   keep   you   down?
It's   only   right   that   you   should
Play   the   way   you   feel   it
But   listen   carefully
To the sound of your loneliness
Like   a   heartbeat   drives   you   mad
In   the   stillness   of   remembering   what   you   had

And   what   you   lost
And   what   you   had
And what you lost ·

Oh,   thunder   only   happens   when   it's   rainin'
Players   only   love   you   when   they're   playin'
Say   women,   they   will   come   and   they   will   go
When   the   rain   washes   you   clean,   you'll   know
You'll know

Now   here   I   go   again
I   see   the   crystal   visions
I   keep   my   visions   to   myself
It's   only   me   who   wants   to   wrap   around   your   dreams
And   have   you   any   dreams   you'd   like   to   sell?
Dreams of loneliness

Like   a   heartbeat   drives   you   mad
In   the   stillness   of   remembering   what   you   had
And   what   you   lost
And   what   you   had
Ooh, what you lost

Thunder   only   happens   when   it's   rainin'
Players   only   love   you   when   they're   playin'
Women,   they   will   come   and   they   will   go

When the rain washes you clean, you'll know
Oh, thunder only happens when it's rainin'
Players only love you when they're playin'
Say women, they will come and they will go
When the rain washes you clean, you'll know
You'll   know
You   will   know
Oh, you'll know

The Chain by Fleetwood Mac

Listen to the wind blow, watch the sun rise
Running in the shadows, damn your love, damn your lies

And   if,   you   don't   love   me   now
You   will   never   love   me   again
I   can   still   hear   you   saying
You would never break the chain (Never break the chain)

And   if   you   don't   love   me   now
You   will   never   love   me   again
I   can   still   hear   you   saying
You would never break the chain (Never break the chain)

G. Keller

Listen to he wind blow, down comes the night
Running in the shadows, damn your love, damn your lies
Break the silence, damn the dark, damn the light

And   if   you   don't   love   me   now
You   will   never   love   me   again
I   can   still   hear   you   saying
You would never break the chain (Never break the chain)

And   if   you   don't   love   me   now
You   will   never   love   me   again
I   can   still   hear   you   saying
You would never break the chain (Never break the chain)

And   if   you   don't   love   me   now
You   will   never   love   me   again
I   can   still   hear   you   saying
You would never break the chain (Never break the chain)

Chain keep us together (running in the shadow)
Chain keep us together (running in the shadow)
Chain keep us together (running in the shadow)
Chain keep us together (running in the shadow)
Chain keep us together (running in the shadow)
Chain keep us together (running in the shadow)

I finally clicked off the stereo.
I listened to the sound of loneliness.

But   listen   carefully   to   the   sound
Of   your   loneliness
Like   a   heartbeat   drives   you   mad
In   the   stillness   of   remembering   what   you   had
And what you lost, and what you had, and what you lost.

I was going to sell all of Mom and Dad's clothes at Sharon's Riches. Everything. And I was going to fix this house—myself.

They broke the chain, and I have a new dream, a dream that doesn't include them.

Chapter Forty

I felt empowered organizing my inventory.

I spent the next week putting mom's things in groups: coats/jackets; blouses; handbags; belts; shoes; pants; shorts; dresses; ball gowns; sporty stuff; jewelry. I did the same with dad's stuff. I pulled out all the tagged clothing from the six wardrobe boxes and added them to my organized groups. Within each group of items, I divided them in half: tagged and untagged.

Then I got a spiral notebook and began listing the items by number, gave a detailed description, and included the designer's name. Mom had taught me very well about fashion, and I knew what looked good together, so I decided to pair dresses, shoes, and handbags into outfits that looked stylish. I had little piles neatly stacked all over Mom's old bedroom.

The week went by so quickly with my new summer routine: swim and shower at the clubhouse; eat the latest gluten free pastry left in my locker by the clubhouse chef; and spend all day inventorying my parents' precious things. So precious at the time of purchase, only to be easily cast aside when they were of no use anymore. Wasted money.

I felt no remorse getting rid of everything. In fact, it was liberating.

Chapter Forty-one

Friday came and I had selected beautiful items to take to Sharon's. I used a medium box, and everything fit fine in it. I showed the bus driver Sharon's Riches address on the business card the pawn man gave me and asked if there was a bus stop close to it. Lucky for me there was. I didn't have to walk across the tracks or watch jets fly away.

Sharon was so excited to see me when I walked in the door. "I sold the dress, shoes, and handbag! $2,200!"

I could hardly believe it. I set the box down and she hugged me. I was so startled I just stood there stiff in her brief embrace.

"I usually take 40%, but if you have clothes as unique and stylish as that gown, I will only take 35%.

You won't get a better deal at any other consignment shop in Portofino."

Of course, I had no idea if this was a good deal or not. I should have gone over to Starbucks this week and done some research, but I didn't want to bump into Brianna and Langston again. And besides, I was overwhelmed organizing my parents' things.

I quickly did the math in my head. I just made $1,430! I was sitting on a gold mine and my body flushed with excitement.

She handed me a check. Oh no. My face must have looked disappointed because she said, "Is that not enough?"

"Oh no. It is fair…I guess…I don't really know…but I…. but I," I couldn't think of a lie quick enough so I blurted, "Could I have cash instead of a check?".

She paused a moment, digesting the request, and replied, "I guess so." Took the check back and tore it up while walking over to the cash register. She dumped the check pieces in the trash, wrote something in a check ledger, and pulled out several one-hundred-dollar bills. Fourteen of them to be exact. Along with a twenty and a ten.

As she counted it out in front of me, I almost started to cry, but instead, I forced a smile and crammed the money into my wallet and zipped up my backpack.

"Let's put your backpack in a safe place for the day. Bring your box and follow me."

We walked to the back of her store past a beautiful curtain separating her workspace from the elegant shop. She opened a locked cabinet, and I put my backpack in it. Then we opened my box.

I brought four dresses with handbags and shoes to match:

A blue and white floral casual dress by Eskandar with strappy black Saint Laurent sandals and a black Salvatore Ferragamo handbag; an exquisite Marchesa Notte floral dress with embroidered flowers at the hem with a pink Giuseppe Zanotti leather flower high heeled sandal and a pink Dolce and Gabbana handbag; and two beautiful Badgley Mischka dresses – one pale blue with a deep V-neck, sleeveless and pleated to flow easily and the other a sequin lace racer halter dress in pale peach with an ivory lace overlay. I paired both dresses with beige Jimmy Choo strappy heeled sandals which looked almost identical and had no idea why mom would need two pairs of shoes that looked the same. I picked a Yuzefi white and gold handbag for the blue dress and Jimmy

Choo nappa leather clutch with a crystal bracelet handle for the lace dress.

After I laid each carefully coordinated ensemble on the workroom table, I stood back and admired my selections. I looked over at Sharon and she looked speechless.

"I don't quite remember how my mother wore these dresses. Do you think these shoes and handbags go together?"

"I am enchanted," Sharon uttered. "I told the lady that bought your mom's other dress, shoes and handbag to come in today because I would have some nice new inventory, but I had no idea how lovely the clothes would be. And the shoes. And the handbags. Do you want to display the dresses, and I'll look up prices? The woman is bringing her best friend. They usually come in around 11 a.m. and then go to lunch. These ladies are my best customers. They love getting designer bargains. They could go to the most expensive stores in town – and probably do – but coming here is unique. They like the unexpected."

There were several elegant mannequins lined up against a wall. I began to put the dresses on them like I saw Sharon do it last weekend. She smiled in approval and wrote down prices on tags. She carefully pinned the string on the tag inside the back label of each dress, and then gently wrapped tags with strings around the handles of the handbags and the straps of the shoes. I looked at each tag and gasped at the prices she wrote down.

"Will people really pay this much for a used dress?"

"Not just any used dress. These dresses are not in circulation anymore and were created by top designers. They are like art. And these ladies coming in have more money than they know what to do with. A thousand dollars to them is pocket change. Shopping in my store is fun for the super- rich because they never know what they are going to find. That brings them some excitement. Like finding a treasure at an antique or art auction."

"Are all of your clients super rich?"

"Oh no, I have those who want to *pretend* to be super rich too. The wannabees. They can find a dress that retails for $1,000, pay 3 or $400, and then walk around Fifth Avenue like they own the place."

I thought 3 or $400 seemed like a fortune, too, for a dress. Spending this kind of money on clothes was ridiculous, but right now, I am glad someone was. It meant air conditioning. It meant running water. It meant food in my mouth.

Sharon carefully opened each handbag to double check if they were empty. I had made sure of that before

I put them in the boxes, but I saw her open a side zipper inside the Jimmy Choo leather clutch. I hadn't noticed it had a zipper inside. Sharon pulled out something.

"These must be your mom's. Wow," she stared at a plastic looking card. "She looks exactly like you. You could be twins."

She handed me mom's driver's license and a light blue card that said social security.

"Those are important. Put them in your backpack and don't lose them," she added as she checked the other handbags only to find them empty.

Why wouldn't mom take her driver's license and social security card with her? Did she not only leave me, but change her identity too? Why would she do that? How could she do that? This was so upsetting........ I had to stay focused and not think about it, about her. I needed to stop letting her moral deficiencies keep ruining my life. I was finding a way to move on, and I needed to shake her off.

"What else can I help you do?" I asked, changing the subject.

After we displayed the clothing in the front windows, Sharon looked me up and down.

She had a disapproving look. "Hmmm, you can't wear that."

I didn't even think about what to wear today. I was so busy organizing Mom's stuff and trying to stay cool. I had on gym shorts and a flimsy old t-shirt and ratty sneakers.

"I don't care what you wear on a regular day. I know teenagers wear bummy clothes, but when you come work for me, I need you to look classy."

"I'm sorry. I have nicer clothes." And I did. Mom used to buy me equally expensive clothes before the 'incident' and even for a time after. I was really thin right now, however, and slightly taller. I ate sparingly and swam every day, so I'm sure clothes from sixth and seventh grade still fit.

I used to tell Mom to stop buying me clothes, but she said I needed to look sophisticated now that I was becoming a young lady. She always bought me the latest styles for teens, too. Not stuff she would wear. She made sure that I was not only sophisticated looking but young and hip. I always thought my mom bought me those clothes so that I looked good standing next to her, like a mini-Victoria James. I wasn't surprised when Sharon said we looked like twins. People always said we looked alike. But now, after all the inventory work I had done this week – and I wasn't even through half her stuff- I realized she had a shopping problem, an expensive shopping problem. Some people were addicted to alcohol or gambling, but my mom was clearly addicted to shopping. And just like other addictions, it destroyed our family.

When things got tougher and Mom started working at McCormick's—a discount designer warehouse, she would bring home some nice things. Not the top designers like before but sometimes little treasures of cool stuff. Mom really knew fashion. And she just couldn't stop buying clothes. That must be why she left us. She liked things more than people. More than Dad, more than me.

Now I needed to get rid of every greedy garment she ever bought.

"I promise I'll wear a nicer outfit tomorrow."

I hadn't dressed up since Mom and Dad left. I wore the same jeans and T-shirt or shorts and T-shirt almost every day. I was washing a few shirts in the sink of the clubhouse, wrapping them in a towel, and hanging them in Mom's courtyard, out of view, to dry. I had three outfits I kept revolving. When the clubhouse was closed for remodeling, I just took them to the shutter house and hosed them in a bucket of soapy water and rinsed them out.

"I don't think I have anything for you today in my store. Most of my clothes are for a more mature clientele, but I do want to start a younger line of items, so if you want to sell any of your things, let me know. Today, though, you'll have you work in the back when the ladies get here."

I hadn't thought of selling my things, but I loved the idea. I suddenly didn't want to wear anything Mom had ever bought for me. If Sharon wanted me to look nice, I would save a few things, but that was it. "I would love to sell my clothes, too. I have very nice things. I could help you make the teen corner very cool."

"Great!"

Then I had another idea. "What about men's clothes? My dad has some nice suits. We could put a male mannequin next to the female like they are going to an elegant party?"

"Wonderful idea. Are you sure your dad won't mind?"

"He won't mind." Why would he mind? He never wanted those fancy suits anyway. He never wanted the fancy house, the fancy cars, the fancy shoes, ties, parties.

He would want me to eat – right?

***

I was in the back when I heard the doorbell tinkle open, and Sharon turn on the charm. I thought she was nice to me, but when I heard her start talking to these high roller clients, she sounded overly gregarious.

"Charlotte, look at these dresses!" A lady exclaimed with delight.

Charlotte replied, "My Lord, I've never seen anything like them. Jewel, look at these handbags and shoes!"

"Is this from the same lady I bought the dress from?" Jewel asked.

"Why, yes, it is. She goes straight to New York, London, and Paris to do all her shopping, and even meets personally with designers who sometimes make clothes just for her. She has so many clothes that her husband told her to get rid of some or she couldn't shop anymore. Even though I think he is a prince or something and she could buy as much as she desired. So, I am the lucky recipient of her impeccable taste and one-of-a-kind wardrobe. She told me she would bring me a few things each week this summer. So, you will have to make me your Friday or Saturday stop," Sharon said.

Who knew Sharon could tell lies and so smoothly. Lies to make more money. You rascal Sharon. The two ladies drank in her tale with excitement.

"She also told me that all the money she makes from selling her clothes here, she is giving to charity. Isn't that so wonderful? It's like when you buy her clothes, you are giving to a good cause," Sharon sweetly said.

"How thoughtful and generous of her," said the Jewel lady.

"Charlotte, we are going to have to fight for this blue pleated dress. It would match both of our eyes, and wouldn't our husbands love the plunging neckline?"

"Jewel, we are so lucky we are the exact size of this woman. Even the same shoe size."

"Sharon, what is her name? We might know her. Although, I have never seen these clothes on anyone here in Portofino. Have you Charlotte?"

"No."

Sharon interjected, "My client wants to remain anonymous. She spends most of her time in New York and Europe. She is only here a few months out of the year. Right now, they are renovating their mansion in Port Royal, and she is having her maid clean out her things."

Wow. The lies were getting bigger. It made me wonder about Sharon. I wanted to like her because she was helping me sell my stuff to make the money I desperately needed, and she was super nice to me, but maybe it was an act. Like how she is feeding these ladies lie after lie. Maybe she is like everyone else – Mom, Brianna, Langston – just using people for their own gain, and when that relationship didn't benefit them anymore, they bolted. Yea, I needed to keep Sharon at a distance. Purely professional. She was a way for me to make money. Best not get too close. When I was done with her, *I* would be the one to leave.

"I bet I know her. You know the new wife of that prince from Egypt. We saw her once at the Children's Charity Fundraiser. She was breathtaking. And so mysterious. Remember her? She is hardly ever in town."

The two women seemed to get a thrill from trying to act like they knew this made-up mystery lady.

Charlotte and Jewel wanted all of mom's dresses, shoes, and handbags. I heard Sharon begin negotiating money. Then Sharon told them to sit, and she would bring them a glass of champagne while she boxed up the items.

When she came to the back room, I raised an eyebrow. "The wife of a prince?"

Sharon smirked and whispered, "Hush. I create an experience. They come back because shopping here is unique and interesting to them. Don't mock me. I sold all your things. And they got into a playful bidding war for that blue dress and Charlotte paid me almost double what I wrote on the ticket. This is a game to them. Money is their toy." She popped a bottle of champagne and poured it into crystal flutes.

I heard her voice go animated again. "Here you go ladies."

She came back instantly while I heard the rich ladies laughing and having fun. I couldn't help but think that is what my mom desired. Champagne, shopping, and shrieks of laughter. Not a care in the world except what to spend their money on and where to go to lunch.

"Let me show you how to package the items. I like the people who shop here to think of this experience as a special occasion, so I always wrap everything like an expensive gift." She reached under the table for some nice glossy white boxes that said 'Sharon's Riches' in gold cursive on the top. She carefully put the shoes in shoe boxes and the handbags in separate boxes. She wrapped one box in wide gold ribbon and showed me how to make a perfect bow. I grabbed a box and copied what she did while she transferred the dresses from the mannequin to a wooden hanger. Then she carefully wrapped each dress with a white traveling cover that zipped up the middle.

All this time she worked slowly and methodically. "Never rush. These ladies have nothing to do, and I want them to enjoy themselves." She grabbed the champagne from the ice bucket, disappeared back out front and asked Charlotte and Jewel, "Would you ladies like more champagne?"

They giggled like little schoolgirls, "Why yes!"

Sharon worked out in the front part of the store while the ladies talked. And the more they drank, the louder they got.

"Sharon, can you believe that Jewel's husband never locks the doors to their house during the day? And they live right on the beach. People walk up and down that beach all the time. He thinks it is 1955," Charlotte was practically shouting.

Jewel started laughing, "He is so old and just doesn't think anyone will break in. He said he never locked his house growing up and that's how he likes it. He wants to be able to walk in and out during the day without worrying about locks. I told him one day we will come home, and everything will be gone."

She continued, "No cameras, either. He is convinced the government is spying on everyone and will hack into them and watch us. Like we are so exciting. We even have a large safe in the master bedroom closet in plain view full of cash. And he leaves that open, too. He doesn't even pay attention to what he puts in it. And he forgets everything. I told him the housekeepers are going to start stealing from him if they haven't already. I swear. The older he gets, the crazier he gets!"

Sharon just laughed along with them and said it was sweet that her husband wanted to live like simpler times.

The conversation infuriated me. How could people with so much be so careless with their money? I was struggling to figure out how I was going to eat, and they were sipping champagne and laughing about leaving their mansion unlocked and their safe open with thousands of dollars in it. Of course these two loved my mother's clothes. Jewel and Charlotte were just like her. No respect for money. Look at all mom spent on useless things. Things that have no purpose but to look good. How vain. She had no respect or regard for money and neither do these women.

I decided I didn't like Jewel and Charlotte.

Chapter Forty-two

By the fourth of July, I had made $8,365.

The first thing I did was take my old cellphone to Verizon and got on a prepaid plan. I would call Lorenzo Williams Technical High School after the holiday and give them my new phone number.

Then I fumbled through the box of mail on dad's old couch and found an electricity bill and a water bill. I called them, and they told me I had to come down and pay cash if I didn't have a check or credit card. I remembered when mom and I had that disastrous day selling dad's bike at the pawn shop and then slinking over to the utilities building to turn our electricity back on. Taking the city bus system was easy now, and I had no problem getting down to the south side of town. When I stood in line, I watched the people. Most looked really hard up for money. A tired mom with a crying baby, a middle – aged man who looked defeated, a heavy older woman who seemed out of breath. And me. An orphaned, soon—to-- be 14-year-old.

It felt exhilarating to get everything working by myself. I felt stronger and more in control of my life. I bought a hot plate at Target that acted like a makeshift stove top until I finished the remodel. I filled the refrigerator with groceries and began to cook things I hadn't had in a long time that were easy and I loved: spaghetti and meat sauce, tacos, chicken and rice, and ice cream. I loved mint chocolate chip ice cream. The cool, creamy treat tasted fresher and sweeter after living on peanut butter and bread for the last few months.

Even though I had running water at home, I continued to swim at the club every day because I had fallen in love with it. Something about the rush of water against my skin took me to a different world, void of sound and distractions. And I loved holding my breath and seeing how far I could swim underwater without breathing. When I finally reached the surface, I would grasp a giant breath of air like I was a baby taking my first breath.

That night, I sat out on the patio staring at the night sky, waiting for fireworks to start filling the blackness and thinking, *I can do this. I can survive on my own.*

Roach Girl origin trilogy one

Chapter Forty-three

Jewel and Charlotte were Sharon's best customers. I always managed to stay in the back when they came to the shop. Occasionally, I glimpsed at them from behind the curtain, but I never went out to meet them. I told Sharon I was too shy and too afraid I might mess up her elaborate lie. She agreed I should remain silent in the back.

Jewel and Charlotte were both tall and thin. Jewel had let her hair turn gray and styled it in a swept back flip that came shoulder length. She wore thick, black framed glasses and today she was dressed in a crisp white button-down blouse with a bright blue, pink, and gold paisley silk scarf tied around her neck. Her wide beige trousers rested high on her waist with a belt made of the same fabric cinched to accentuate her trim figure. Her open-toed heels were the same color as her trousers, giving her an elongated silhouette.

Charlotte was equally classy. She continued to dye her hair chestnut brown and casually tied it in a thick bun at the nape of her neck. She wore a body-hugging floral dress in shades of pink, white and orange. Her delicate sandals had a tiny heel and sparkly jewels stitched on the strap.

I peeked at them from time to time to put faces with their often-outrageous conversations. I knew everything about them after one month. I knew they both married men over twenty years older than them and were second wives. They seemed to think that was funny, laughing about how they stole these rich men from their wives and family. Then started new families with them. I knew Jewel had twin daughters when her husband was 65 and she was 43 and they were now seniors in high school—which made her 61 years old and her husband 83. And that they *would* spend the summer at their cottage in Maine, but her daughters rowed Crew and were training with their coach all summer. So, Jewel was stuck in this God forsaken swamp until August and would only get to spend one month in Maine before having to return for the girls' senior year.

Charlotte sympathized with Jewel's plight like it was so rough to only get to spend a month in Maine this year but assured her that next year the girls would be off to college, and she could do whatever she wanted. They both clanked champagne glasses to that. I learned Charlotte had one son when she turned 40 and her husband turned 60. And that her son was 25 and working in New York. They had a second home in North Carolina and flew back and forth from spring to fall and then stayed here permanently all winter. I learned Charlotte wasn't in North Carolina yet because they were renovating the mountain house, and it wasn't done yet. Even though Charlotte's husband was now 85, he still worked and ran a huge corporation. Thank God, according to Charlotte, otherwise their marriage would be doomed. Having the old man around 24/7 would send her over the edge.

I also learned that both ladies shared the same plastic surgeon, and I must admit, he or she must be fantastic because Jewel and Charlotte looked very young for being in their 60s. I didn't see them up close but could tell that they did not look their age. Sharon asked them one Saturday how they managed to look so young, and Charlotte said they stayed out of the sun and that even though they both live right on the beach, they never went outside without a giant hat and tons of sunscreen. Maintaining their appearance was their number one job.

It is what landed them their husbands and their fortunes, and they couldn't lose that.

I learned that their mansions on the Gulf of Mexico were exactly one block south of the pier and that Jewel's mansion had an enormous patio recently added around her Olympic size pool. And Charlotte's mansion was two doors south of Jewel's and had a pool with an enormous fake mountain waterfall that she detested because it looked like a tacky resort at Disney World. But her husband loved it and told her she couldn't change it. His grandkids and great grandkids from his first marriage loved sliding down the theme-park style slide in the middle of the mountain. Jewel empathized with this apparent world – class tragedy, having to put up with fake mountain pools and grandkids from first marriages.

With each conversation I overheard, I detested these ladies more. Their worlds were so easy that they had to make up stupid crap to worry about. There were people all over the world without food to eat, and Charlotte's biggest worry was having a pool that looked tacky—and Jewel's biggest worry was being stuck in her Florida mansion all summer and not going to her Maine house. I wonder how they would feel if their rich old geezer husbands died and left them penniless. What would they do? Sell the mansion on the beach? Go back to work? Could they survive?

Charlotte and Jewel were just like my mother. If the money ran out, they would run out. That is how they would survive. By finding another rich old man to fill their empty, materialistic souls. Yes, these women were just like her.

And I hated them all.

Even though I couldn't stand Jewel and Charlotte, Jewel did help get my teen corner off and running by bringing in tons of her twin daughters' clothes. Her daughters' clothes, added to my things, started an influx of teen clothes from moms making their daughters clean over the summer. I was super busy organizing all the new inventory. We didn't take everything brought in. If for some reason we didn't like it, we told clients we had too much inventory but would give it to charity if they wanted. As a result, only outstanding pieces of clothing and shoes were on display in the teen corner. Girls started making Sharon's Riches a summer hot spot of activity.

And mom's gems continued to be the highlighted beauties showcased in the storefront windows along with a recently purchased male mannequin sporting dad's suits. Weird. Looking at the store front window was like staring at a plastic mom and dad.

I was helping Sharon make a fortune, and all this time, I remained busy and hidden in the back of the store.

I dressed classy like Sharon told me to, but I didn't want to converse with anyone. I was only there two days a week and was too busy sorting and organizing to chat with people who came into the store. Sharon was so good at schmoozing. Best leave it to her.

And I was super grateful for that when I heard the doorbell tinkle open and a voice I knew exclaim, "Mom, look at all this cool stuff."

Brianna.

Chapter Forty-four

My heart started racing, and I jumped behind a large wooden wardrobe armoire. My eyes darted for a quick exit, but the only way out was through an emergency door that might set off an alarm. Sharon was out front and would start talking to her soon.

"Mom, I want this dress," barked Brianna to her mother.

I couldn't hear what was being said next because I was hiding. Muffled exchanges. I heard Sharon's animated happy voice but couldn't make out what she was saying either. Hopefully she wasn't saying the dress belonged to a girl named Vivian.

It seemed like an eternity went by, and finally Sharon walked back with a dress in her hands looking around for me.

"Vivian, where are you?"

I had slunk to the floor trying to disappear into it. I looked up at Sharon. I must have looked terrified and pathetic because her voice softened, and she crouched down close to me.

"What is it honey? Why are you hiding back here?" She glanced at the curtain separator and back to me. "Is it that girl? Do you know her?" Sharon had sharp instincts or maybe girl intuition or something.

"Yea, I went to middle school with her. We used to be friends. She turned on me," I spoke the truth without giving too much away. "Don't tell her I'm here." I looked at the dress Sharon was holding. "*She* wants to buy *that* dress?" I spat in a whispered rage.

"Yes, why? Is there a problem?" Sharon said.

"Last fall my mom bought me that dress, um, before she died," I quickly recovered my lie, "for the eighth-grade dance. I knew she probably spent her entire paycheck on it, but it was so gorgeous, and I thought my boyfriend would like it. I took a picture of it and showed it to Brianna. She said it was ugly, and I would look terrible in it. She said it was out of style. I was stunned. My mom never bought things that were out of style, and it confused me. The part that I hate is I believed her and didn't wear it. I told my mom to take it back…. but she didn't. Brianna is now dating my old boyfriend. She is a mean girl. I hate her." I couldn't believe how much truth I was spewing at the moment.

"Ok, stay here. I have an idea," Sharon left, and I heard her go into her act.

The dress was spectacular. I remember when my mom brought it home, how in awe I was. I had tried it on, and it fit like a glove. Mom had been so excited because it was an Oscar de la Renta dress, and she couldn't believe her good fortune, finding it on a shipment before it was put out on a rack. Oscar de la Renta dresses rarely found their way to McCormick's. She had said it would retail in the thousands. The pale blue dress had beautiful flowers in pink, white, yellow, and orange embroidered with delicate green stems all over the dress. It fit tight at the bodice with a sheer see-through mesh laid over the strapless bodice and flared gently at the waist, giving a fairy tale princess look. Mom had been so disappointed when I told her I wasn't going to wear it. I remember her face looked hurt. Now I realized that Brianna just didn't want me to wear it because it *was* spectacular, and she didn't want me to look good.

"Honey, I am sorry about this dress, but it is sold. My partner just got a phone call from a young girl who was looking at it this morning, and she paid with a credit card over the phone. I am so sorry for the confusion, but this dress isn't available." Sharon's lies were effortless, which was a bit worrisome. What else could she lie about? But at this moment, I didn't care. She was my hero.

Brianna's mom's voice sounded relieved. "Honey, you will have to pick out something else."

Sharon came back and laid the dress on the table and winked at me on the floor still hiding.

After looking around some more I heard Brianna say, "Let's go to the mall."

The doorbell tinkled and they were gone.

***

Sharon walked back and lifted me off the floor and gave me a hug. "I hate mean girls," she whispered in my ear. Even though I didn't want to trust Sharon with her slick, expensive appearance, her beauty, her effortless ability to lie, I couldn't help but like her.

"Vivian, you need to keep this dress as a reminder to never let girls like her make your decisions for you," she let go of me and pulled out a white box. She carefully folded the dress into it and tied a beautiful gold ribbon around it and handed it back to me.

***

On the bus ride home, I was feeling empowered again. Sharon was right. I wasn't going to let people like Brianna or Langston or my mom or my dad bring me down. I was a fighter, and I was winning. I wasn't going to hide behind a cabinet and cower to anyone. Roach Girl was stronger than Country Club Girl. I was surviving and thriving. I had a job with money coming in, I figured out how to pay the utilities, my refrigerator was full, and I was going to a high school far away from Brianna and everyone.

As I walked home from the bus stop with the white box in my arms, my heart clenched in sudden alarm as I saw a large enveloped taped to my front door.

I peeled it off and read the return label. Kearnst and Pearson, PA.

I fumbled to unlock the new handle I installed on the front door and shut the door behind me. I ripped open the envelope.

We were being sued. By Royal Palm Estates. For unpaid homeowner's dues. $18,565. Pay by October 31 or the house will be owned by development.

Chapter Forty-five

For the second time in one day, I slunk to the floor and wanted to melt into it. Why is life so hard? Just when it seems like you are seeing the light at the end of a dark tunnel, someone or something boards up the exit. Where is that strong Roach Girl? Where is that 'never going to cower on the floor again' girl I had pumped up on the bus ride home? Gone. Evaporated with one white envelope.

What am I going to do now? I was about halfway through mom and dad's clothes and even if I sold everything and made the same amount as I did with the first half, it would only give me another $8,000 or so. Not enough. And that wouldn't even happen anyway because I took all the best stuff to Sharon first. The remaining clothes were nice, but not the artistic one-of-a-kind selections that I had been selling.

And I was hoping to use the money I was making on keeping the luxuries I needed to make life more bearable: electricity, water, phone, food. I thought if I was frugal, I could keep the place comfortable until I learned how to fix the house and sell it.

Now, if I didn't figure something out, I would lose everything. End up in foster care, living in some shanty on the scary side of the tracks.

My eyes filled with tears, and I started crying, heaving style cries where your whole body gets into the sorrow. I couldn't stop. My hands were shaking. An avalanche of tears wet my face and snot clogged my nose. Damn. Everything is so hard. I get it now. Why mom left. Why dad left. Life is just miserably hard. It is so easy to just walk away when it looks like you will never get out of your mess.

So why am I not just walking away like they did? Why am I still trying to hang on?

Foster care might not be that bad. Maybe I would live with someone like Sharon. But wasn't Sharon just like Mom, Charlotte, Jewel, Brianna, Langston? She looked like them. Shiny and slick. But she felt nicer somehow. I don't know who to trust. She acts nice but looks like them. And she lies, little lies, but still. Who knows what big lies lurk around the corner. Get real Vivian. She is probably a phony like all the rest. People like Sharon don't take in foster kids. Their lives are too busy with parties and charity events and fancy ladies and champagne. And laughter. Who wants the burden of taking in a homeless teenager?

So why am I not walking away like mom and dad did? Why am I still trying to hang on?

Because I am not Country Club Girl. Country Club Girl would walk away and look for an easier life. But I am not her. Not anymore. I am Roach Girl. And Roach Girl can withstand anything – being crushed and humiliated and lonely and broke and tired. Roach Girl can survive the most difficult circumstances, making her stronger. I sat up and began calming down, wiping my face with my shirt, and beginning to breathe rhythmically. Yes, get it together Vivian. Get it together Roach Girl. You are indestructible. You can do this. Think.

Chapter Forty-six

One thing the papers from the lawyers said was that we, or I, couldn't use the clubhouse or any amenities until the homeowner dues were paid in full. So that meant no more swimming laps in the pool. The pool had become my peaceful place. Until I came up with a plan to pay back all the money to Royal Palm Estates, I couldn't swim.........or could I? Portofino lies on the banks of a giant pool—the Gulf of Mexico. And Sharon's Riches was just a few short blocks from one of the world's most sought-after swimming destinations.

I decided that on Friday I would ask Sharon if I could leave work a couple of hours early, so I could walk over to the beach and go for a swim in the Gulf before taking the bus back home. Friday was my birthday, and I longed to just get in the water and swim until I was out of breath.

***

When Friday came, I put a swimsuit, change of clothes, flip flops, and a towel into my backpack. I decided to tap into my parents' jewelry drawer and go back to the Priceless Pawn to see if I could raise more money for the unpaid homeowner's dues. I grabbed the two items I thought were the most expensive: my dad's Rolex watch and my mom's pearls. The Rolex didn't work, but I knew it was expensive. Dad had gotten mad at mom for buying it. He said a Rolex watch was impractical. They weren't reliable timekeepers. Mom argued it was more like jewelry for men and that who cared if it didn't tell good time, he could look at his phone for the time—a Rolex told people you had made it.

For a moment, I wondered why they left such expensive things if they weren't coming back. But then I remembered that these were gifts they had given each other. And they had given up on each other. So why *would* they keep them.

Well, I had given up on them, and I didn't want their stupid jewelry either.

I needed the money to pay for their mistakes.

***

The Priceless Pawn guy's name was Roy. Roy offered me $900 for the Rolex and $300 for the pearls. I was hoping for more, but what choice did I have. I knew that even if I sold every single item that belonged to my parents, I maybe could come up with the money for the homeowner's dues, but what about other bills? They would just keep coming in. I would have to continue to pay the homeowner's dues monthly, along with the electricity, water, phone bill, and groceries.

Today, I turned 14 and should be celebrating with friends and my family, but celebrating was the last thing on my mind. I needed to figure out my life and how I was going to make all this work. Although I was lucky that Sharon gave me a job, the money I earned at Sharon's Riches barely paid for groceries. The real money was in the items I was selling, and once I was out of items, I was out of money – again.

My eyes wandered around the pawn shop. It was my birthday. 14. Normally, I would be getting presents. Even in our dire straits, mom always managed a present or two. She was a great gift giver. As I looked at used, pawned items, I realized how pointless material crap was. People think they need a new dress or new shoes or a new car, but do they really? No. And when they tire of the momentary thrill of owning something new, it sits in their closet or garage until they get the urge to buy something newer or run out of money and have to come here and pawn it. Why? Why do we feel we have to own this crap? I suddenly felt disgusted by all of it. All I wanted for my birthday was for my chest to stop feeling tight. I wanted my family back. No present wrapped in a pretty bow. Just a happy family with no problems.

As much as I hated my mom and my dad for leaving me, I would be overwhelmed with relief and joy if I went home today, and their cars were in the garage. I wonder if they were thinking of me today. Of the day they brought me home from the hospital. Dad used to tell the story right before we lit the candles on my cake every year. *"It was 4:00 in the afternoon on a Friday and your mother had just eaten a piece of pizza. You weren't due for another ten days and after one piece of pepperoni, your mother started to feel sick. We thought it was indigestion and didn't think too much about it. Then, your mother kept feeling sick and we thought we should go to the hospital just in case. On the way there, your mother started having severe contractions. I had to speed up like in the movies and start running red lights. Your mother said, 'don't kill us on the way to the hospital,' and I raced to the emergency room. Your mother was fully dilated at this point and the emergency nurse screamed 'don't push'. Within minutes they had your mother in the room, and you were born six minutes after arriving at the hospital. The best day of our lives."*

Really? The best day of your life? How good could that day really have been? How could dad feel that way and then leave me 14 years later? How could mom buy me presents and throw me parties and make me believe I was special all these years and then walk out?

Maybe it was possible that one of them would choose today to return. Maybe. But I wasn't going to get my hopes up. And I wasn't going to buy myself a gift. I was going to swim at the beach for my birthday and let the cool, salty water melt away my worry.

After my transaction with Roy, I walked across Airport Road to go straight to Sharon's. I had to pass through the unsavory neighborhood, as my mom would have called it, again. The bars on the windows and junky yards scared me less now. So much had happened over the past three months that I didn't really care and wasn't scared of much anymore. My pace was deliberate and determined and purposeful and as I passed a bright yellow house, my thoughts were deep, always planning my survival.

In the periphery of my thoughts, I heard the bouncing of a basketball. I glanced down the driveway of the yellow house and saw a tall boy shooting hoops. I slowed for a second when I realized who it was and before I could dash away unseen, he saw me too. Leo from Lorenzo Williams Technical High.

I tried picking up my pace to pretend I didn't see him, but it was too late. "Hey, you are the Beachside Girl." He jogged towards me.

There was nothing I could do but stop. "Yea, hey." Awkward silence followed as I tried not to look at him.

"What are you doing here?" He asked bewildered to see me. "If you wanted to check out the high school, it is over that way," he pointed the opposite direction, "across the street from the executive airport about two blocks. Are you lost?" He still looked incredibly confused to see me, and I was shocked to see him.

"Do you live here?" I asked, impulsively changing the subject until I could think how to answer. "Yea." He answered sort of breathing heavy from exercising and without shame or embarrassment. "I suppose it isn't the castle you come from." He smirked playfully.

The house was so tiny, it looked like Leo would have to duck to get through the front door. But even though the house wasn't much bigger than my garage, it was neat and cute. Red and blue flowers were planted in parallel rows adjacent to the sidewalk that led to the front door. The lawn was thick, green, and mowed. White shutters decorated two large windows and the whole yard had a white picket fence along its perimeter. Yes, this was a loved house.

In fact, it stood out like a beacon of light along the street, and I remembered noticing it on my last walk from the Priceless Pawn to Sharon's. It stood out amongst the sloppy houses with long, weedy yards, barred windows, mildewed roofs, and chained-up dogs that scared most people in neighborhoods like these. If all houses looked like Leo's, this neighborhood would not be scary to anyone.

"Actually, I work at a dress shop over that way," I pointed west. "I am just addicted to pawn shops and took the bus to the Priceless Pawn before my shift starts." All of this was sort of true.

His eyes scaled my image quickly drinking in my statement. I suddenly remembered how elegant I was dressed, and I had been styling my hair now, too. Sharon insisted I look chic. I was wearing a knee-length white dress with spaghetti straps and cinched at my waist was a matching white belt. I wore tan wedge-heeled sandals that wrapped up the lower part of my calf. I had been swimming so much that my body was glowing, fresh pinky-brown and my blonde hair was lightened with natural sun-streaked highlights that looked better than any expensive salon could create. I am sure I looked like the last person addicted to rummaging through a pawn shop. I recovered quickly, "I collect vinyls. You can sometimes find some treasures at the pawn shop. Nothing today though."

There was another awkward pause. I had a hard time looking at him and found my eyes fixated on his house instead. He wasn't wearing a shirt and the sweat from a midsummer day in south Florida made his caramel-colored body glisten with sweat, and although he was lean, he was very muscular. My heart was speeding up, and I was certain my face was red. Hopefully, he would think it was just the heat and my tan.

"Well, have you seen the school yet? I can walk you over there after you get off work. Show you around," He was so nice. "It's not open, but I can show you what it looks like from the outside."

"I actually brought my swimsuit and was going to go to the beach for a swim after work," I said. "Maybe another day." I meant it, too. I was very curious about the high school. The school that was going to teach me how to remodel my house. But today was my birthday, and all I wanted to do was swim and swim and swim in a pool so large I could swim forever if I wanted.

"OK," he said.

"Well, I better get to work," I started to back away and turn towards Sharon's.

"Hey, why don't I join you at the beach?" He called out as I was walking faster away.

I wanted to swim alone, but I had been alone so much that it might be fun to have company. And he seemed so nice. And it *was* my birthday.

"Ok, meet me at Sharon's Riches at 4:00," I called and turned away.

"Where is that?"

"Straight across the tracks. You will find it."

I couldn't help but smile a small smile.

Chapter Forty-Seven

"Can I help you?" Sharon's cheery voice sounded less animated and more real. As soon as I heard the other voice, I realized it must be 4:00.

"I'm here to see......," Leo had a casual, comfortable tone and vibe, always, but I could tell he suddenly realized he didn't remember my name. "Beachside girl."

I walked out from the back where I always worked in sheltered anonymity. "Hey."

I had told Sharon a friend was meeting me here to go to the beach, and she let me store my stuff in the back room.

She smiled at both of us and said, "Have fun. I'm closing the shop at 7:00 so be back then."

As soon as we were out of the store I said, "It's Vivian. Call me Vivian." I didn't want any pretentious nickname. I would have been OK with Roach Girl but figured that would take too much explaining.

"Ok, Vivian."

***

As soon as we got to the beach, I disrobed my t-shirt and shorts, ran past Leo, and dove without hesitation into the waves. When I popped up for air, Leo was right next to me shaking his big head of hair. He ran a hand over his face to wipe the salty water from his eyes and flashed an enormous white smile.

"Feels great."

"It does," I agreed.

We sort of floated and bobbed with the waves until Leo challenged me to a race. He pointed to a distinguishable mansion with a top floor observation deck and said, "First one to that mansion wins."

Before I could ask 'wins what' he starts the challenge, "On the count of three.... One, two, three, go!"

We took off in a splash of excitement. I plunged underwater, held my breath, and swam at lightning speed. When I popped up, Leo was right next to me again. "Tie." He said laughing.

We floated along catching our breath, drifting, and talking. I kept the conversation light, avoiding any talk of parents. I asked him about the school and the teachers. He loved his school and spoke highly of everyone. Leo was one of the calmest, kindest people I had ever met. While our conversation was easy, we both avoided eye contact. As if eye contact might trigger something we weren't ready for.

My leg accidentally brushed his and a jolt of electricity shot through my body. "Sorry," I whispered.

"It's Ok," he smiled and let his body rise to the top of the water, so he was floating gently, sort of making an ocean snow angel.

I looked over at the enormous homes on the beach as we swam leisurely back to our original spot. I couldn't help but think how real it felt being with Leo. He didn't care about clothes or jewelry or popularity or living in the biggest house on the block. He just enjoyed being. It exuded from him. He radiated peace, and I was drawn to him like a moth to a bright light. I had a sudden urge to touch his hand but didn't. I never felt this way about Langston. I had forced myself to like him, as if liking Langston was the right thing to do – to gain some sort of status. He was so concerned about being cool, wearing the right clothes, having the right hair, dating the right girlfriend. He was tense and uncomfortable to be around. If my hair wasn't right or my clothes weren't right or my lunchbox wasn't right, I was not worthy of his affection.

Leo was the opposite of Langston....... Or was he? How could I really know? Leo knew I was from the north side, that I went to Beachside Middle, that I lived in a fancy house, that I wore fancy clothes, and maybe his desire to come to the beach today with me wasn't any different than Langston's. Maybe Leo was taken with my outward appearance and status just like Langston. I looked over at him, risking eye contact. He looked directly at me with eyes so blue they battled the water and sky for brightness. Could those eyes be shallow or were they as deep as I desired them to be? How could I really know after one afternoon at the beach? I looked away, but I felt his eyes still watching me.

Disappearing under water, I held my breath and swam away, gracefully reemerging with more distance between us. He swam closer, closing my newly formed space, and our hands brushed under water. This time he took it and held it. I didn't know what to do. All I had wanted for my birthday was to swim forever in hopes of forgetting about everything, but now my chest was pounding so hard, and I was anything but calm...... but I liked it.

Until this moment, I didn't realize how alone I felt. I had a sudden urge to lean into him and let him wrap his arms around me and hold me and tell me everything was going to be OK. That I didn't have to worry anymore. That he would rescue me from this nightmare I was trapped in.

He must have sensed this and pulled me up close to him. He let go of my hand, and I felt both of his arms wrap around my waist and lock behind my back. Without hesitation or permission, he gently kissed my lips and let go of his hands on my back. This was exactly the way I dreamed my first kiss would be—at the beach with a handsome boy. Not the gross closet kiss on a dare in a friend's bedroom. As far as I was concerned, this was my first kiss. The other one didn't count. The other one was forced on me by peer pressure. It wasn't a kiss. It was a duty I had to perform to keep my Country Club Girl status with Langston and the rest of them. This was my first real kiss. A kiss we *both* wanted.

One hand found my hand again. The other hand touched my face. Our feet were sinking into the sand while the waves rocked our bodies back and forth.

"You are so beautiful," he said to me looking directly into my eyes.

With those words, something snapped, and I pulled away. Dramatically, I dove into the water to swim away. I knew he would follow. What could I say to him? I couldn't get involved with anyone right now. I couldn't. And all he knew about me was that I was pretty. Was that all he liked about me? It didn't matter anyway. I was living alone and had a mission to complete. I didn't need someone to rescue me. I could rescue myself. Leo would only complicate things for me, and my situation was embarrassing.

When I resurfaced, he was right there again. "Hey, did I say something wrong?" He grabbed my hand and wouldn't let go, but in a kind way, not aggressive.

"You don't even know me," is all I could think of saying.

"True, but I want to know you more."

"Why? Because I'm pretty?" My voice had an edge.

"I'm not going to lie to you and say I don't think you are gorgeous, because you are. But there is something more to you. You are not like other girls. I mean..... A Beachside kid leaving a top-rated school district with fancy everything to come down here to high school to be a builder? I have been thinking about you ever since I met you. And then you randomly walk down my street. I couldn't believe it when I saw you today," he paused, staring at me. Then continued, "There is more to you than most girls. I didn't mean to imply I liked you just because you are pretty. I'm sorry. Kids from Gulfside High think they are better than everyone, and you want to leave them. I like that. I like you because you are different.... bold."

Why did he have to say the exact right thing? He pulled me close again and with our faces centimeters apart, he whispered, "I just want to know you more. I'll take it slow." He gently brushed his lips on mine. Then he backed away and dove into the water away from me.

Awkward silence followed.

Take it slow. I could do that. Maybe things at home would get less complicated. Maybe.

I changed the subject and pointed to a modern castle on a private peninsula, "Look at that. What do you think the price of that place is?"

He looked over and said, "Oh, we call that the point palace. My mom and her cleaning crew clean the place. I've heard kids try to swim out there, but I think it is just talk. My mom said she has never seen any kids come close. I don't have any idea how much a place like that costs. A lot. Mom said a prince owns it."

There was a rocky barricade surrounding the yard protecting the palace from the waters yet leaving a stretch of white sand, giving the rich residents their own private beach. It almost looked like an island, but a tiny strip of land connected it to the mainland. You could see a tall gate keeping people off the peninsula.

I turned away and noticed another beachfront mansion. A home with a huge tacky theme park style pool, and I forgot all about Leo's blue eyes or the point palace. Charlotte. I remembered her complaining about it. I looked at the home two doors down from Charlotte's and noticed a beautiful Olympic-sized pool. Jewel. I couldn't believe their homes. How could they complain about anything? Not being able to vacation in Maine this summer? Really?

Suddenly my thoughts were consumed with my reality. My horrible reality. My brief respite from my nightmare instantly over. Look at the people in this town and how they spend their money so lavishly. For the price of one mansion, I am pretty sure you could feed several countries for several years. How can people do that? Drop money on expensive clothes and shoes and cars they don't really need when so many people in the world are hungry? I wonder if Jewel and Charlotte gave money to hungry people. Or do they say they will and go shopping instead?

Then I remembered something Jewel said about her old husband always keeping the doors unlocked. The unthinkable entered my mind. How could a girl with straight A's, perfect attendance, from the north side of town, have a thought like I just had? But I needed money to survive, and I was trying so hard to keep everything going. Would Jewel's husband really miss a little bit of cash? Would it really affect their lives if something went missing from that mansion? I hated the thought. I hated myself for thinking the thought at all. But....I had to survive. I had to get out of the debt I was drowning in. I had to do what my parents couldn't do. I had to. I was obsessed with fixing the problems my parents created and then left me with. I wanted to show them I wasn't a quitter. I had more strength than they had. I was tougher than them.

Could I really do it? Maybe. I don't know. Probably not. But maybe I could. Like Robin Hood. Take from the rich to feed the poor – the poor little roach girl.

***

It was a thought.... a back-up plan......one that was now in my head, and I couldn't get rid of.... like a roach infestation......

Chapter Forty-eight

For the rest of July, I went back to riding the bus to Sharon's Riches without the Priceless Pawn detour. I was avoiding walking past Leo's, not because he did anything wrong, but because I had other obsessions bigger than him. Survival takes up all the space in your head. Getting involved with Leo would only complicate my life more than it already was and distract me from my goal. When he asked me for my phone number, I told him I was getting a new phone and didn't have a number yet.

But at night, when the house was dark and quiet, and I played music softly, my mind reenacted the kiss. Over and over in my head, I visualized Leo and his beautiful body and piercing blue eyes. I visualized his face coming closer to mine, and our lips gently touching, our hands gently touching, our bodies gently touching.

What an unexpected day that was. I thought it was going to be my first birthday alone, but it wasn't. It was my first real kiss. A day I wanted to forget turned into a day I would never forget.

But I kept my thoughts of Leo just that. Thoughts. Fantasies. I couldn't risk a real relationship. I had too many home problems to solve.

***

Jewel and Charlotte hadn't been to Sharon's, and I waited with nervous energy for them to make their grand entrance. I wanted to get a nugget of information about their plans or daily schedule. As time passed, a full-blown foolish fantasy filled my lonely nights with make-believe entertainment. I forced thoughts of Leo from my mind and instead pictured myself a stealth, agile thief in a black tank swimsuit gliding through dark waters like a purposeful porpoise, then slinking alongside a Port Royal mansion and slipping through unlocked sliding doors. A modern-day Robin Hood. A good thief. I was about to give up on this insane idea of stealing from them when they marched in on the last Saturday in August.

"Sharon, anything fun I can take to Maine?" asked Jewel. "I leave next week. Or perhaps something for tomorrow night? Charlotte is throwing my husband and me a going away party. I could use something new."

I almost laughed out loud at that ridiculous statement. Since when does Jewel or Charlotte or anyone else in their circle of acquaintances need something new? Get it straight Jewel. You *want* something new. Needs and wants are very different things. Food is a need. Water is a need. A dress is not a need unless you don't have anything to wear. *Anything.* She needed to go back to second grade economics. That is what these two grown women sound like. Second graders who just must have a new toy.

"Charlotte, when do you want us to come over?"

"Let's watch the sunset before dinner. How about 6:30?" Charlotte suggested.

My heart pulsed with the information.

Could I make my fantasy a reality? Could I steal and get away with it? Could I steal and not feel riddled with guilt?

Maybe.

Chapter Forty-nine

My house was infested with roaches and my mind was infested with sinful scheming. That night I couldn't sleep. I put the Rolling Stones on the CD player and listened to *Beast of Burden* and *You Can't Always Get What You Want* on repeat. I watched a roach crawl across the wall. I might have electricity and water now, but the roaches haven't gone away. I thought of getting a few roach hotels, however, a couple of scattered poison squares would hardly do the trick on this army of insects.

I didn't really care anymore. All I cared about tonight was whether or not I was going to steal from Jewel. Everything I had ever been taught growing up told me stealing was horrible and how could I even harbor the thought for more than two seconds. But during all these lonely, hot summer nights after swimming with Leo at the beach, I had been having these fun fictional fantasies about becoming a modern-day female Robin Hood, taking from the rich to give to the poor – starting with me—poor little roach girl.

I pictured how I would do it over and over in my head and it was fun...... when it wasn't real. Like I was writing a script for a crime series and the main character was good and evil mixed into one, and the audience would be debating after the show about the ethical and moral justifications of her actions. Some would tout me as a hero and others a villain.

It was fun when it was fake. But now I had the notification from the lawyer in my hands staring at me, yelling at me to pay $18,565 or lose the house. I can't lose the house. I have gone through too much to give up now-- starving, sweating, defecating and bathing in bushes, roaches swarming my body, being humiliated and left alone.

I finally figured out how to survive and then this. Another obstacle. An $18,565 obstacle. And I have a plan to fix the house. A good plan. An honest plan. A work my tail off plan. I'm going to school to be a carpenter, plumber, electrician, and architect just to make this all better. I am not a lazy criminal just wanting to steal to go buy a new TV or piece of jewelry. Useless crap. I need the money to live here because I have nowhere else to go.

I'm *not* a criminal. But what if I get caught? Would I go to jail? How horrible. No, I wouldn't go to jail. If Jewel and her husband caught me in their house, I would tell them I broke in to steal a beer on a dare from my friends. I would tell them I was dared to drink it in the closet and take a photo to prove I did it. I will wear my most expensive bathing suit, and one look at my long blonde hair and trim tan body in that expensive suit, will make that old-fashioned man think back to his younger days when he did pranks with his friends. I'll plead innocently and muster up some tears and say I'd never do it again. Jewel won't recognize me because I never showed my face at Sharon's Riches. And she is so into fashion, that one look at me and she will think I live in the neighborhood somewhere. I'll look on a map for a street name a few blocks away from Jewel that I can rattle off my approximate fake home location.

I made a decision. I would follow the plan I had rehearsed over and over in my head, and when I got to Jewel's mansion at 7:00pm tomorrow night, if I couldn't do it, I would just come back home.

No harm in a late-night swim in the Gulf of Mexico for a tough girl like me.

I watched the roach on the wall take its time creeping to a corner as if it knew it wasn't in any danger of being squashed. I listened to the Rolling Stones and thoughtfully closed my eyes, breathing deeply, going over my plan again and again in my head.

"Ain't I hard enough…..ain't I rough enough…..ain't I tough enough….Put me out…put me out…..put me out of misery."

Was I tough enough, brave enough, crazy enough to do this?

Yes. I was. Tough like that crazy, brave roach waltzing across my wall in wide open view. Jewel and her husband had more money than they knew what to do with. What was $18,565 to them? Pocket change. Pocket change that would change my life for the better. Wouldn't they want that? To have their money help the poor? I would just be taking from someone that probably wouldn't even miss it.

Taking from the rich to give to the poor. Remember, Robin Hood was a hero – right?

Robin Hood? Roach Girl? Heroes. Not thieves.

Chapter Fifty

Isolation transforms you into a master of imagination. A fantasy world is a survival technique. It manifests once basic needs are met. Once you have hunger controlled and the necessities taken care of, your mind needs taking care of....and that is where imagination offers its services. If you are not careful, it can turn into a runaway train—first it helps you get through the night, like a train transporting you from night to morning light, but if it goes too fast and too determined, it can pick up speed and run into the daylight, not stopping, gaining speed to the point where the only way to stop it is to crash or hang on tight and hope the train runs out of gas and slows to an easy stop.

My imagination had turned into a quest I can't explain, a bullet train. I carefully prepared for my day, leaving nothing to chance. I wore the most expensive bathing suit I owned under a flimsy t-shirt and barely there shorts. On my feet, I wore aqua socks, which can be worn to walk on or swim in. In my small backpack, I put a large plastic Ziplock bag, rubber gloves that my dad had in the garage, and regular socks. I had already checked to see if everything fit into my backpack, once rolled up tight, and it did, easily. So, I knew if there was cash added to the bag, it would fit.

At 5:30, I slipped out the door and knew exactly how to get out of Royal Palm Estates undetected by cameras. Next to the maintenance offices, I had discovered a space between the brick wall that surrounded the neighborhood, and the building that housed all the lawn mowers. One Saturday after grocery shopping, I biked past the maintenance people cutting down a large, dead tree, exposing the opening. They planted a new tree, but it was small. I could easily slip in and out of the neighborhood there. And since it was Sunday, no one would be working in maintenance. And since it was August, few lived in Royal Palm Estates.

The bus driver was so used to seeing me riding the bus each weekend that he didn't even turn his head to look at me when I climbed on. Once dumped off on the south side of town, instead of turning to Sharon's Riches, I turned towards the beach. The streets were empty as I made my way to the Gulf of Mexico, but if anyone did see me, they wouldn't think twice of a teenage girl with long blonde hair and tan body going for a walk on the beach. I looked like I fit in perfectly.

All the time I spent slinking around Royal Palm Estates when I needed my garden hose shower or outdoor toilet or to fetch much needed water, prepared me for the stealthy movements needed to go undetected once I approached Jewel's mansion. I took off my t-shirt and shorts, stuffed them in my backpack and began walking the beach. Just another person going for a sunset stroll. When I got to Jewel's, I looked at the house and froze. I couldn't do this. I couldn't....... but I had to. I had to, to survive. I needed this money to live. They wouldn't even miss a little cash. It wouldn't adversely affect them at all. Once I had everything paid off, I would never do it again. I could even pay them back one day, when I sold the house, so it was more like a loan.

This last rationale gave me the needed courage to take another step.

I walked a little further down the beach to Charlotte's house and crept up the side of the backyard. There was a giant hedge, but I could hear them all laughing. I knew the time was perfect. They had all started dinner. Now or never.

It was dusk and the beach was vacant. I slipped down two houses along tall hedges until I got to Jewel's backyard. I crouched and opened my backpack, exchanging aqua socks for gym socks. I didn't want to leave any prints. I slipped on rubber gloves with shaking hands. Without hesitation, I swiftly whisked along the sliding doors of the back of the house and opened the first door I tried. Jewel wasn't kidding. Their house was easy to get into. And just like Jewel said, not a camera in sight. My midnight fantasies had become reality and my heart raced. I quickly opened the fridge to see if there was beer. Bingo. I grabbed a bottle in case I got caught. I was sticking to the teenage prank excuse for being there.

I gingerly crept around the first floor. I figured their bedroom was on this level with the old man being in his eighties. He wouldn't want to go up and down the stairs much. My heart was pounding so loud I had to quiet it by swallowing, which seemed like an exaggerated motion. I found the bedroom and the 'his and hers' closets. I had to breathe deeply to stave off panic.

Then I saw it. The safe. Cracked slightly open. I looked around me. The house was silent. I set the beer on the floor next to the safe. I opened it. I couldn't believe what I saw. Stacks of cash. Stacks and stacks of cash. Was it real? It almost looked fake, like play money your mom gives you when you are little to play grocery store with. There were stacks of hundred-dollar bills, too many to count. I decided to take just three stacks. I didn't want anything to look out of the ordinary. I was afraid if I took too much, they would notice. I didn't take time to count how much was in each stack. I was too nervous. As I reached for the bundles, I noticed my hands shaking wildly. I shoved the stacks into my backpack. I looked at the rest of the cash in the safe. It didn't look like anything was out of place. Good. I carefully closed the safe door to exactly the same position. I started to leave and then remembered the beer. In my heart-racing urgency to get out of there, I almost forgot it. That would have been a disaster.

Next, I tiptoed around looking for a window to unlock. The house may be open now, with them staying here, but when they leave for a longer duration, those doors will most likely be locked. Next to their bedroom was an office that faced the beach. There were French doors and two windows flanking each side. I slipped back the lock on one of them and tested to see if it opened. It did. I closed it back up, but left the lock unlocked—in case I needed to come back and get more money. There was a good chance this window would get locked back up before they left, but I probably wouldn't be back anyway.

I walked to the kitchen and put back the beer.

Once out of the house, I slipped quickly behind a hedge next to the beach and sat down, hidden from view.

I took off my socks and gloves and stuffed them into the backpack after taking out the plastic bag and aqua socks. I put the aqua socks back on and rolled the backpack up as tight as I could and zipped it in the plastic bag. Smoothly, I vanished into the water, swimming north.

***

That night I couldn't sleep. What had become of me? A thief? Me? Country Club Girl? I wasn't a thief. I wasn't. I couldn't believe I had reached a point where I would stoop to a level of crime. I wasn't a bad person. I wasn't. I shouldn't have done this. What was wrong with me? I had become despicable. I suddenly hated myself. There were other options. I could have told Sharon what was going on and maybe she could help me. I could tell Leo and maybe he would help me. There were options – legal ones. Why did I choose such a horrible solution as this?

I would find a way to pay them back. That's it. I would fix what I had done. Once I paid the homeowners' dues to keep my house. Once I figured out a legal way to make money. Once I sold this house. I would pay them back. I would.

My body started to relax. My breathing started to calm. I reached over to my portable stereo and turned on the Rolling Stones. *You can't always get what you want........You can't always get what you want........You can't always get what you want.....But you get what you need.*

My eyes started to droop, and I drifted into a dreadful dream. I had turned into a roach. An actual roach. My body contorted like the man morphing into the Hulk, but instead of turning into a muscular green giant, my eyes bulged into large, sinister spheres. Exaggerated long antennae sprouted from my head and strong indestructible wings burst out my back. Jagged appendages replaced my arms and legs creating a grossly fierce, evil, ugly creature. I flew and crawled frantically, trying to get away from something – I couldn't tell what-- something trying to hurt me. My body twitched like a dog in a nightmare until I woke in a sweat. I was breathing so hard my chest heaved. I tried to slow the wild breathing. My eyes opened, and I focused on the ceiling....... where a roach clung motionless.

Chapter Fifty-one

I had been too nervous to even open my backpack last night. I hid it under a loose board in the vacant room adjacent to my parents' bedroom that was supposed to be an office, but you couldn't tell with just framing for walls. I had wild thoughts last night on the bus ride back. It was late, and I had never ridden the bus back that late before. There was a driver I didn't recognize. I pretended to act normal, staring out at the night streets, but inside, my heart was wild with thunder. I imagined every worst-case scenario. What if Jewel and her husband went to get money out of the safe to take on their trip to Maine? What if they recognized the money was missing? What if the police investigated the city buses for unusual riders at night? What if they came to my door with police dogs?

In the morning, I decided to go see how much money I had taken.

$15,000.

Crap. Not enough. I was $3,565 short.

***

I debated all week about what to do. I went over the remaining clothes in mom and dad's closet and knew I didn't have enough to make that much. Reality started to hit me. Even paying the past due homeowner's bill, I would need approximately $1,500 a month to keep everything working in the house and the new homeowner's dues paid. When school started in two weeks, I would only be able to work at Sharon's on Saturdays, earning enough to buy me groceries for the week. How was I going to pay for everything else?

I decided to go back one more time to get another $15,000 to pay back homeowner's dues and survive until I could figure out a way to fix the house and sell it. Then I would pay back Jewel with the profits.

This time I didn't go to Jewel's at night. I decided to steal in daylight. I was going to do exactly what I did last time, but on a regular bus route. So, everything looked normal.

On Friday, I asked Sharon again if I could go swimming at 4:00. I told her I didn't need to come back for anything because I would just throw my shorts back on and head home afterwards. I changed into my lucky bathing suit at Sharon's and started walking to the beach like any normal teen.

When I got to Jewel's, I surveyed the house by slipping up the side to the front, hiding along a tall hedge. The place was deserted. I opened my backpack, put on gloves, and changed into socks. Before I lost my nerve, I walked to the back of the house where the office was and tried the window I had left unlocked. It opened. I looked around. No one in sight. I hurdled the window ledge easily and was in. Hurdling walls had become second nature to me.

I grabbed the beer just like before.

When I got to the old man's safe, it wasn't open this time. But when I pulled the lever, it opened.

Nothing.

Crap.

I started looking around for something else that was valuable. Something I could maybe pawn for money. My heart was racing again. I opened every drawer of a tall cabinet in the closet. There must be something. I looked around at the expensive clothes and shoes. I could take something to sell. Jewel wouldn't be back until late September. I'm sure we would sell it by then. But as nice as these clothes were, that idea seemed impractical and difficult to pull off. How would I lug bulky clothes in and out of this house and not get caught? I was tired. I wanted an easier fix. A faster fix.

As I stared at the shoes, trying to think, I saw a tiny green corner of a bundle of money. Excitement filled my veins. I grabbed the shoe and there was a stack of money shoved in the toe. I started to look deep in the toe of all the shoes. Money in each one. What was the old man thinking? Hiding money in his shoes? I grabbed another three bundles but realized that there was a stack in each pair of shoes. He would notice missing money if three shoes were empty when he returned. Then I counted how many pairs of shoes there were. Twenty-two pairs of shoes. That is forty-four shoes with cash. Would he miss the money if I took two pairs of shoes? What if he just thought 'there is money in each pair' so when he returns, he just looks for money in each shoe?

I decided to shove two pairs of shoes, with bundles hidden in them totaling $20,000, into my backpack.

And before I could change my mind, I put back the beer, looked out the window to see if anyone was there, and slipped away.

***

When I got home, I took the old man's shoes out to the garage. Looking around for a way to destroy them, I settled on a pair of hedge clippers. I began hacking. And the more I hacked, the more I liked it. I hacked the old man's designer shoes into tiny, unrecognizable chunks of leather. Bottled up anger made me unable to stop. Anger towards mom. Anger towards dad. Anger towards money, abundance, greed. Hacking felt exhilarating. Hacking felt liberating. Hacking felt powerful. I couldn't stop. I stared at the pile of leather confetti scattered in a rage-infused disorganized pile, my chest heaving with adrenaline.

I wanted to hack something else. Walking back into the house, I went to the bathroom and stared at myself in the mirror, clippers dangling at my side. The face staring back at me looked so much like hers, and suddenly, I hated it. I wanted to hack off all my hair. The hair mom wanted me to highlight. The hair Langston liked straighten and smelling perfect. Mom's hair. I put both hands on the hedge clippers and maneuvered them, so a giant chunk of blonde hair hung between the long blades ready to float to the floor.

Then I stopped.

No.

I wanted to have short hacked-off hair in the worst way. I wanted to look completely different than her. But if I cut off my hair, it would draw attention to me. I remember taking the suicide prevention course last year in health class. One sign that a kid is suffering is a drastic change in appearance. I couldn't have Sharon or Winston or Leo or Mr. Rexford alerted to the possibility that something was wrong with me. I had to keep everyone believing life was just fine here. I couldn't have anyone come snooping.

Chapter Fifty-two

On Monday, I called the phone number on the overdue homeowner letter from the attorney and pretended to be my mother. The man told me they would accept a check or money order and gave me the address where to send it. I then asked the man if I could pay in advance for the next five months, and he said yes. I asked the exact total for the late money and the next five months, and he paused to calculate. $21,565. That would leave me $13, 435. Enough to keep my phone, electricity, and water turned on and groceries for several months.

Then I would figure out a way to pay back Jewel.

I searched on my phone places where I could purchase a money order since I didn't have a checking account. Little red flagged markers popped up all over

Portofino. I enlarged the map, and a familiar place came into view.

The Priceless Pawn.

I didn't want to wait until Friday when I worked at Sharon's. Having all this cash in the house made me uncomfortable.

***

When I walked through the door, Roy was at the counter.

"Hi Roy, I need a money order," I said as if we were close friends, although I don't think he even knows my name. But I knew he recognized me by his tone.

"Sure, do you have the name and address of where to send it?"

"Yes," and I got out the letter and five bundles of cash.

Roy froze. And looked at me hard. "We cap money orders at $1,000. You are better off going to your bank and getting a cashier's check."

My turn to freeze. I didn't have a bank account. Awkward silence hung in the air as I stood there without a solution.

"I suppose I could do several separate money orders. How much cash is this?"

"$21,565," I stated flatly.

Roy raised an eyebrow and started tapping the counter with his pen.

"Ok. I'll do 22 money orders totaling that amount. There is a $2.00 fee per money order. I also need your driver's license."

I didn't think about needing ID. In my panic, I instantly remembered something. My mom's license and social security card I had put in the zippered pouch of my backpack and never took out.

With as much confidence as I could fake, I reached for mom's license, praying he didn't ask me any questions.

He looked at the picture on the license and back at me. "Victoria James." I could tell he was skeptical even though the picture could have easily been me. Then he sighed like he didn't really care. He took the license and wrote down something on a form and told me to sign. I counted out $21,565 and then an additional $44 for the service fee. Good thing I brought extra cash.

I signed, Victoria James.

He gave me a receipt.

When I got home, I took mom's license and social security card out of my backpack's side zipper and stared at it.

Then it hit me.

If this stolen money gets traced, they will look for Victoria James….

What have I done?

Chapter Fifty-three

The school bus was scheduled to arrive at 5:50 a.m., and I made sure I was at the guardhouse early. The transportation lady at Lorenzo Williams High thought the guardhouse was the safest place for me to stand that early in the morning, and since no one from my area went to this high school, there wasn't a designated bus stop.

The sky was pitch black with thousands of stars glittering the sky, shining in such a distance, they did little to lighten the earth, but looked amazing. I kept craning my neck to gaze at the wonder. A strange, eerie feeling lingered inside me. I felt like I was slipping away from society, utterly alone. Like the sky was about to suck me up into orbit where I would float, lost in space among the unreachable stars.

Thankfully, Winston emerged from the guardhouse and waved 'hello', as I waited under the faint, orange glow of the streetlight, just steps away from him. The darkness and silence, as I stood with my backpack, felt less lonely knowing he was just a few quiet feet away.

Breaking the stillness and the blackness was an abrupt emergence of distant yellow and orange lights. A beastly vehicle, snorting and breathing deeply, lumbered down the road towards me. I knew this was my ride. It halted to an abrupt stop. The driver pulled the lever to open the door, and I climbed onto the empty bus, sliding into a seat about eight rows behind the driver. He pulled the door shut and looped around the guardhouse, chugging back the way he came. We cruised down the same road the city bus had taken me all summer to the Priceless Pawn and Sharon's Riches—a road I had memorized. A road that took me to my new life.

No one else boarded the bus the entire way. I had a giant yellow limo ride by myself. The sun started to light the sky to a dull gray and when the bus turned left on a street directly across from the executive airport, I couldn't help thinking about the day I went there and saw mom getting on that jet with the old man. I would have to pass this place five days a week. I had to be reminded daily of her deserting me. Uhg. Another pang of loneliness pierced my heart.

As the bus slowed down the quiet street, I saw a bum shuffling along the sidewalk covered in a dirty, burgundy, oversized hoody, blanketing his entire body. I wondered how he could even see with the hood pulled down so low. He was pushing a shopping cart, and I couldn't help but think how hot all those clothes must be.

We passed more run-down houses.

As we neared the school, my mood shifted from melancholy to nervous. I forced a mind shift, telling myself that this school was the answer to my problems. This school would help me. I closed my eyes and envisioned a completed home, a home with classic hardwood flooring, creamy custom kitchen cabinets, shiny faucets, sparkling light fixtures, smooth vanilla-painted walls, glossy crown molding......... a beautiful home. A home *I* finished.

I suddenly felt a little more empowered. At this school, I would be learning what I needed to finish the house. And I had a desperate new reason to accomplish this goal: I needed to sell it to make a profit and pay back Jewel. I owed them $35,000. I wasn't a thief. I *would* pay them back. I was certain that a finished remodeled house in Royal Palm Estates would sell for a good price.

I was also nervous about seeing Leo. I figured he would track me down at Sharon's, so I told her to tell him I wasn't there if he came in—and he had---twice. Both times, Sharon gave her over-the-top performance lie that I had called in sick. The second time he asked for my phone number. Sharon eloquently said she wasn't allowed to give that information without permission. He understood and left his number in hopes I would call him.

I never called.

I wanted to.

Desperately.

I thought about him every night as I lay in bed listening to music and the faint sounds of my little roach friends scratching across the walls. I thought about his lips brushing mine and the taste of warm, salty water on his skin. I thought about his hands brushing my thigh and then finding my hand to hold. Sweet. Innocent. I re-enacted my first *real* kiss over and over and over in my mind. I was embarrassed I hadn't called him. What was he going to do when he saw me? Would he be upset? Would he snub me?

Now I was nervous to see him. It was the first day at a new high school. What could I say to him? Sorry I haven't called. I've been too busy with my second job—cat burglar.

As the bus pulled up to the school, kids were gathered near the front door. Butterflies fluttered in my stomach. The driver opened the tall, folding door, and I took a deep breath and descended.

There, like a lighthouse in a sea of students, stood Leo, looking straight at me, his eyes shining brightly, guiding me to safe waters.

Chapter Fifty-four

Lorenzo Williams Technical High School was a beautiful brand-new looking school in the middle of a working-class neighborhood. It was much smaller than the traditional high school I was zoned for, and I loved it immediately.

When I got off the bus, Leo was warm and kind and never asked why I hadn't called him, which was a relief and made me like him even more. He gave me a friendly, gentle hug, and his smile was effortless and comfortable.

"How was the bus ride? Long?"

"It seemed fast to me, but I'm a bit nervous."

"Don't be. Everyone is cool here." He paused. "We have time. I can give you a little tour if you want."

I nodded yes nervously while holding the straps of my backpack, giving my hands something to do.

He showed me an open area where kids learned to fix airplanes, and I was in awe at the three small jets out in the open. I had never seen that at a school before. There was another area where students fixed cars, and then an entire hallway with large rooms where kids learned the building trades. Next, he took me to the cafeteria and asked me if I wanted to meet him there for lunch, and he would introduce me to some people. I replied a relieved 'yes,' and then we headed back to the front office area where Leo told me I would be getting ninth grade orientation.

"See you at lunch," he smiled and turned, slipping into the crowd.

***

Everyone at LWTHS ate a free lunch. This was awesome. I didn't have to worry about bringing a lunchbox. I would be able to save money on food, so I could pay Jewel back faster. I wanted to spend as little of the remaining money I had stolen as possible.

The morning flew by, and I found myself searching for Leo in the cafeteria. He appeared out of nowhere and guided me through the lunch line and over to a round table where some kids were already gathered. Leo introduced me to Fish (Casey Fishburne) who was in the culinary program; Dexter who was in the building program like Leo and me; Macy, Leo's sister, and Kendall, Macy's best friend, both surgical nursing students. They welcomed me to the group, and I began to relax as they started talking about assignments and internships with excitement. No gossip or drama. They seemed like nice people with their eyes set on their futures. They didn't even act surprised when I told them I was in the building program. Dexter just said, "Cool."

The day went by with lightning speed, and as I found my bus to go home, I heard a call.

"Hey……. Viv," Leo smoothly bellowed.

I stopped and turned on the first step of the bus. "Oh, hey. Thank you for everything today, showing me around and meeting your friends."

"No problem. Hey, I was wondering. Friday night my parents are having a party for their 25th anniversary, and I want you to come. Ask your parents if you can just stay after school with me, and they can pick you up around 11:00," he smiled.

"I don't know. 11:00 is late for my," I almost said parents and remembered I told Sharon my mom was dead. Better keep that lie going. "dad. My mom is dead." This is a problem with lying. You must remember the lies.

Leo's countenance dropped in surprise. "I'm sorry, Vivian. I had no idea." He looked like he didn't know what to say next, so I rescued him.

"It's Ok. It's been a long time. I'm fine. I'll ask my dad," another lie.

Leo hesitated and then recovered his thought. "Just have him pick you up earlier then. Or stay the night? You can stay with Macy in her room. Don't say no. The whole group is coming. My uncle, Nash, is a musician and his band is playing. It is a 60's and 70's theme. And my uncle Jimmy is barbequing, and his ribs have won awards. Just work on your dad this week. It's going to be a blast. He can call my mom if he is unsure about things. Think about it. See you tomorrow." He smiled and turned away.

When I got home and walked through the front door, the house seemed to echo with my footsteps. Echo loneliness and sorrow. Today had been lively and energizing, and now, coming through this door seemed to suck the energy out of me. I had the sudden urge to swim and since I paid up the homeowner's dues, I could return to the clubhouse pool. I threw down my backpack and changed into my swimsuit.

***

I dove in the deep end and swam the entire length of the pool holding my breath. Then back and forth, again and again and again until I was gasping for air, holding the edge of the deep end.

A party.

With Leo and Macy and Dexter and Fish and Kendall. Nice people.

Yes, I would go to the party.

And no, my dad wouldn't call Leo's mom. Permission would not be necessary.

I held my breath and went under again.

Chapter Fifty-five

I loved everything about LWTHS: the kids, the classes, the lunches, the principal, and the teachers, especially Mr. Cooper, the drafting teacher. Drafting class was normally for juniors, but Mr. Rexford approved it because I had taken so many high school classes in eighth grade, I was a straight A student, and I begged. Mr. Cooper was so knowledgeable about construction that I knew he was going to teach me what I needed to know to fix my house. And he was so kind. Every day on my bus ride home, I saw him walk a sandwich out to the bum with the oversized, burgundy hoodie pushing the shopping cart across the street from the school. So cool.

Yes, I liked Mr. Cooper. And Leo was in this class. Extra bonus. I didn't want to complicate my life with a new relationship, but Leo was magnetic.

***

On Friday, I walked home with Leo and Macy. When we got within a block of their house, both sides of the street were already lined with cars. The yard was teeming with people. As we approached, I heard laughing and excitement in the air. There was a happy hustle happening at Leo's house.

Once through the front door, Leo hugged a beautiful woman who looked a lot like Leo, "Hey mom, this is Vivian. She is a new student at LWTHS and is in the building program with me."

His mom wiped her hands on a towel, shook my hand and smiled, "Nice to meet you, Vivian."

There were three other women in the kitchen and Leo introduced them, "This is Aunt Jeannie, Aunt Sue, and Aunt Kathy." They all smiled and said hi.

I could tell everyone was super busy so I said, "Is there anything I can do to help?" The house was tiny, and people had a hard time moving around. I looked through the window and saw all sorts of activity in the very large backyard, people hanging lights, people setting up a stage, people putting chairs around tables.

"Thank you, sweetie, but really, I think the biggest help would be for you guys to go to the beach for a while or something. The party doesn't start until 7:00, and I have plenty of help, so fewer people here right now would be a huge help."

"Ok," turning to me he said, "Did you bring a bathing suit?"

"Actually, I did." I wanted to go to the beach tomorrow after working at Sharon's. I have become addicted to swimming in the Gulf now. The clubhouse pool was fine, but when I swam in the Gulf, the limitless edges gave me freedom I couldn't explain.

"Can you take Jenny and Christopher too?"

"Sure, Mom," and Leo kissed her on top of her head, and I followed him to his room.

As it turned out, Jenny and Christopher were his little brother and sister. They squealed with delight at the idea of the beach. We all quickly changed and headed out the door with beach towels around our necks: Leo, Macy, Jenny, Christopher, and me.

After crossing the railroad tracks, we approached Sharon's Riches. "Let's say hi," I said.

Sharon was delighted to see us. "Hi guys! Heading to the beach I see."

Christopher plunked down in one of Sharon's cool purple velvet chairs and Macy and Jenny started looking at clothes in the teen corner.

"Vivian, I don't need any help tomorrow, but you can come next Saturday." There was a slight edge to her voice.

"Ok," I answered disappointedly. I wanted to make as much money as possible so I could pay back Jewel faster.

Suddenly, Christopher jumped up and shouted, "I have to pee!"

I took him to the back area where the bathroom was located. While I stood outside the bathroom door, I noticed something. There was a folded-up roll-a-way bed against the wall. Strange. I had never seen that before. When Christopher emerged from the bathroom, I looked in. Some personal items were on the counter that had never been there before: toothpaste and toothbrush, hair products and make-up bag. I always thought it was strange that there was a bathroom with a shower in her store. Sharon remarked she liked it in case she had to clean up quick and didn't have time to go home. But this looked like more than a quick change to go out for the night. I glanced back over to the folding bed. Could Sharon be living here now?

Leo was talking to Sharon when Christopher ran barreling out, impatient for the beach now. "I was just asking Sharon to come to the party."

I smiled, "Yea, come."

Leo said, "You won't be able to miss it. Just walk straight across the tracks. It is the yellow house with a white fence and tons of people. My parents invited half of Portofino."

"Ok, I'll come check it out," Sharon said.

***

The beach was a blast and when we walked back to Leo's, the sun was beginning to hang low in the sky. As we approached his house, you could see twinkling lights glowing in the growing darkness and a bustle of activity the closer we got.

Police had the street blocked and I said, "Is there something wrong?"

"Oh no, my dad is a police officer, and he pulled some strings to block off the street for the party. Mom had to invite the whole neighborhood so no one would complain about the noise."

There was a buffet of food set up in the street under a tent and dozens of round tables and chairs for eating. Tiki torches were positioned around the tables making everything look magical.

I used the tiny bathroom sandwiched between Leo and Macy's rooms to clean up and get ready. Leo took his little brother and sister to another bathroom, so they could get ready, and Macy said she would go use her parents' bathroom.

I brought the dress my mom had bought me for last year's Fall Ball at Beachside Middle. The one Brianna talked me out of wearing, but recently wanted to buy. The one Sharon told me to keep for a special occasion.

I couldn't really tell how I looked because the bathroom only had a small mirror above the sink, but when I walked to the backyard, everyone stopped to stare at me. Leo stood in the middle of the crowd and our eyes locked. I couldn't help but feel the energy radiating from him. The yard looked like a fairy tale to me, and when I reached Leo, he whispered, 'You look amazing.' There was a stage set up for the band that was testing the sound. A dance floor had been laid down in front of the stage and white Christmas lights were strung high above the entire backyard in an array that looked like stars dropping from a neighboring universe.

People began flocking in. The band began to play a lively song. Macy, Jenny, and Christopher came running out and started dancing.

"What song is this?" I asked Leo.

"Me and Julio Down by the Schoolyard by Paul Simon. My mom loves Paul Simon," Leo grabbed my hand and pulled me to the dance floor.

The band was amazing. The more people arrived, the more crowded the dance floor became. I decided that 60's and 70's music was the best music on Earth. People were twisting to "Twist and Shout" and "Shake it up Baby". Then two lines formed facing each other and people took turns meeting in the middle and dancing down the center space. I looked across from me at Leo who was staring right back, and I realized our turn was coming up. The song playing was "Low Rider" and Leo and I kept trying to dance lower and lower down the middle until we almost fell. He grabbed me into his arms at the end of the line. We sort of stumbled off the dance floor amongst the giant crowd of people, laughing.

It was dark now, and he held my hand and pulled me off to a less crowded side of the backyard, behind a tree. "I've been wanting to do this ever since our day at the beach this summer." He kissed me softly.

I looked up into his turquoise eyes and got lost in emotion. I kissed him back passionately, surprising myself. It just came naturally with Leo, and he responded instinctively.

Frightened by what was happening, I pulled away looking up at him. He breathed out, slowing down the passion we were both feeling, and took my hand, pulling me back towards the house.

"Come on, let's get something to eat."

The rest of the night was filled with more dancing and singing. Sharon came and so did Mr. Cooper, our drafting teacher. Leo made introductions, and we left them talking when Leo's group of friends came: Fish, Dexter, and Kendall. As the night heated up, people were all singing to songs like "Sweet Caroline" and "She's a Brick House." I had never been around people having so much fun. It was contagious.

"I've never seen you smile like this. I like it. Usually, you are so serious," Leo's eyes were penetrating my soul.

My smile faded, and I remembered reality in that moment, like Cinderella hearing the midnight clock chime and realizing the party's over.

"Hey hey hey. I didn't mean anything bad. You just seem to be having fun, and I like the idea that maybe I had something to do with it. That you like being with me." He pulled me close and hugged me tight.

As I pressed the side of my face to his chest, I felt a tear spring up. Leo sensed it.

"Vivian, I'm sorry. I didn't mean to spoil our fun."

"You didn't. This is the best time I've ever had," I quietly whispered through watery eyes.

***

The crowd slowly diminished.

Our group settled at a large round table and Fish and Dexter entertained everyone with childhood stories. Apparently, they all went to the same elementary and middle school and loved bringing up embarrassing facts about each other. I loved hearing the stories and wished I had been a part of their school experience. Their world seemed more real, relaxed, fun and stress free.

That night, I slept on the floor in a tiny, crowded room with Macy, Kendall, and Jenny, and the next morning I woke to Leo's dad cooking a big pancake breakfast for everyone. Fish and Dexter didn't spend the night, but with all of Leo's family, and me and Kendall, the kitchen table was crowded with people laughing and eating and rehashing the night before.

I watched Leo's mom and dad. Their love for each other was natural. They kissed and hugged, like that is just what they do—all the time---like loving each other was as essential as eating or sleeping or breathing. Their eyes smiled when they looked at each other, and I tried to remember if I ever saw that in my parents. I couldn't recall. I was suddenly overcome with emotion. All the fun and laughing made me realize the void I had in my life, and even though my parents physically left me only a few months ago, they had actually left me long before that. I realized that now. My dad depressed on the sofa, barely moving day and night, barely communicating with me or mom, barely living. Yes, dad has been gone for years. And mom? Mom's robotic movements barely getting her to work and home to sleep, barely able do it all over again day after day, barely uttering a word to me that wasn't an order to clean. Yes, mom has been gone for years, too.

Suddenly, I got up from the table and walked to the bathroom, not wanting anyone to see the tears that were about to escape. Leo knocked on the door.

"Everything OK?" he asked.

I opened the door, "Yea. Let's go to the beach. Just you and me."

He looked right at me and smiled, "I'll change."

Chapter Fifty-six

"Leo, come here a minute," Leo's mom stood in the doorway as we were walking away.

"Wait here," he said to me.

They talked for a few minutes and then she waved and said, "Have fun."

I hadn't been to the beach this early since elementary school and forgot how the water was like glass this time of the day. We waded out slowly, holding hands, and then simultaneously melted into the clear water, both going under at the same time. We were like magnets now, unable to separate. I hadn't realized how much I needed love. My heart was aching with the desire to just touch him and hold him and have him hold me.

We kissed for a while, and then I wanted to swim. I wanted to swim the opposite direction of Jewel and Charlotte's beachfront mansions. I didn't want the reminder that I had committed a terrible crime. But the opposite direction was the Pier and tons of people were starting to crowd that area. So, I pushed back the icky feeling of what I had done at Jewel's and told myself I was paying her back so everything would be OK.

As we swam, I tried not to look at the houses and instead, at the horizon, where boats were popping up. When we stopped swimming, I glanced and saw the tacky theme park pool of Charlotte's house and looked away into Leo's eyes.

We kissed more.

Leo gently pulled back.

"Do you think anyone is there?" I asked, pointing to the prince's palace jutting out on its own peninsula.

"I know no one is there. Besides cleaning houses, my mom also runs her own home watch business for the rich. The prince is one of her clients. He hasn't been there in two years. Since his wife died," Leo said. "My mom checks on it twice a week."

Next to the point palace was a small island with a tiny beach and some mangroves. I had a sudden urge to swim out that far. "Let's swim to that island."

Leo hesitated, "That is pretty far."

"I know." Before he could respond, I was underwater and swimming.

I knew Leo was following. When we reached it, we collapsed on the tiny beach, laughing and out of breath. From the island, I could see the back deck and the pool of the palace. It was magnificent.

Leo pulled me next to him and we started kissing again.

I suddenly felt nauseous and gently pushed Leo away. "I don't feel so well."

"You look like a ghost," Leo looked alarmed.

"I think I need water," I suddenly realized how dry my mouth felt and tried to remember if I drank any water at all since I got up or even last night after all the dancing. "I feel faint."

Leo looked over at the prince's mansion. "I'm going to help you over to the shore of the palace. It isn't far. That place has to have an outdoor spigot somewhere."

I weakly said, "I don't want you to get in trouble."

"Viv, we haven't done anything wrong. We were just swimming to the island. They don't own the island."

I let him put my arm around his neck, and he said, "Hold on like you are riding a dolphin."

I hated depending on him like this, feeling weak, but right now I had no choice. My mouth felt like paste, and I could hardly stand.

He got me to shore effortlessly, and we made our way to the low stone wall that could easily be climbed. Leo hopped first while I held on to the wall. Then he lifted me over.

"Sit here while I scope things out."

Seconds later, he returned. "Found it." Again, he helped me up and practically carried me to the side of the mansion and set me down by a spigot. He turned it on and cupped his hands with water to let me drink it. I started to feel better almost instantly, like a withering balloon that suddenly got a rush of fresh air. I mustered up enough strength to go from his hand-cupped sips to putting my mouth under the water and taking gulps. All I could think at that moment was, 'Here I am again. Slinking around someone's house surviving by using their water spigot.' I wonder what Leo would think of me if he knew I had taken garden hose showers in a neighbor's yard or used the hedge for a toilet. Would he still like me?

Probably. But I wasn't going to tell him my story.

Not now.

Not ever.

We sat perched high on the peninsula for a while looking down at the water and shoreline of palm trees and homes. Portofino was beautiful. And this magnificent home was a masterpiece of construction.

"Do you think we will build homes like this one day?" he asked.

I hadn't thought of it. I was so consumed by remodeling my own house that I wasn't thinking about what I would do with the construction certificate after that. And now that I was looking at this house and the houses along the shore, I knew that building mansions was the last thing I wanted to build. Rich people houses. Second, third, or fourth houses. Poodle baths. Theme Park pools. Fur coat closets.

Those homes were pointless. And I wanted nothing to do with pointless, rich people pleasures.

I could tell Leo wanted to, so I didn't say anything but, "I don't know. Maybe." But I knew when I said it that it was a lie. I did not want to build houses for ungrateful rich people like Jewel or Charlotte or my mom.

I wanted to build houses for people like Leo and his family. Happy people. Small houses. Charming houses. Like the house we owned before we moved to Royal Palm Estates. The house where we were happy.

We got up and walked over to the pool deck to climb the concrete wall. I stopped to look. The pool was so large, and the edge seemed to melt into the ocean. I impulsively wanted to dive in and swim the length. But refrained. It was like my two favorite things – a large swimming pool and the Gulf of Mexico -- had married and produced this masterpiece, and no one was even living here to enjoy it. How can a person build a creation like this and not even live in it?

"Let's get out of here," I said, suddenly revived and anxious to flee.

***

The city bus ride back to Royal Palm estates was long and my mind was filled with a mixture of emotions. When Leo walked me to the bus stop, I wanted to tell him everything. I wanted to tell him about my hollowed-out house, my mom and dad leaving on the same day, living on peanut butter and crackers, selling my mom's clothes to pay bills, listening to roaches in the dead of night.

I wanted to tell him I was alone.

Leo would have jumped on the bus with me or made me stay with him and his family. Part of me wanted that---in the worst way. I knew that Leo's family would take me in if they knew my situation, but I couldn't do that to them. Their house was small, and they already had Jenny and Macy in one tiny bedroom and Leo and Christopher in another. They would probably put me on the couch, and I would be fine with that, but I know it would put a financial strain on them.

And besides, I was a thief. Face it, Vivian. I kept telling myself I wasn't a thief. That I was just borrowing the money. But who was I kidding? I took money that wasn't mine. Isn't that the definition of a thief? Even if I planned to pay it back, the fact is, I took it. How would that look? Leo's dad, a police officer, taking in a girl who stole $35,000 from some rich and powerful Portofino couple? What was I thinking? How was I going to pay them back? Finish my house and sell it? The reality of my situation was sinking in deep on the ride home. Did I really think that I would learn to put in walls and kitchen cabinets and hook up electrical wiring and put in toilets and sinks and flooring just by attending a few classes at a technical school? How immature and dumb could I be? Even if I threw myself into all my building classes, it would take me years to become masterful enough to do this on my own.

My dad couldn't even do it. I remember right after he lost his medical license and they froze my parent's credit line at the bank, dad had just enough money to purchase most of the materials needed to finish the remodel. Stacked neatly in the garage in boxes were kitchen and bathroom cabinets, light fixtures, dry wall, lumber, tools, plumbing fixtures, flooring, and paint. He told mom he would learn how to do everything himself, saving on labor, but he never did. And my parents fought about that, too. And the more they fought, the more dad drank and slept. And never did a thing. If he couldn't figure out how to do everything, what made me think I would be able to?

I could confess everything to Sharon, but yesterday when we were at her shop, it looked like she was living in her store. Did she have financial problems, too? I couldn't be a burden to her. And what about the money I stole – from her client—her best client. If anyone found out, it would destroy her business. And if she was hurting for money, her involvement with me would be catastrophic.

I could just turn myself into the foster care system, but they would send me to live with a family that might not let me work at Sharon's on Saturdays or see Leo….and his family. The foster care people would investigate my living situation and what has been happening to me over the last few months and possibly trace the homeowner's dues payment to the money I took from Jewel. After all, how does a 14-year-old come up with $21,000 to pay off a debt?

My mind was sinking into the quagmire of crap I created. I closed my eyes and rested my head against the glass window of the bus.

Stop thinking. No one has caught me so far. If I could continue paying the bills at Royal Palm Estates, I could live in the empty shell of a house for years. Who would know? The outside of the house looked fine. If it takes years to learn how to remodel this house, so be it. I don't have to do it overnight. I could just keep doing what I'm doing.

No one has discovered me yet.

Chapter Fifty-seven

That fall, I became a Friday night fixture at the Lamonts. Some nights we walked to the beach for sunset, just Leo and me. Some nights everybody went, Mr. and Mrs. Lamont, Macy, Jenny and Christopher and Leo and me. I loved those nights almost as much. The Lamonts had become my part-time family. My only family. They were fun and free of any burdens. Mr. Lamont was a jokester and made everyone laugh. We played Frisbee or football on the white sandy beaches, built sandcastles, and swam in the salty water, watching the orange globe melt into the horizon. We usually stopped at the Twisty Treat on the way back for a hot dog and an ice cream cone.

Leo and his family had accepted me into their clan and for that, I was grateful. Once, when we were crowded around a picnic table at the Twisty Treat, Mrs.

Lamont asked me about my dad. I figured Leo had told them my mom died. I told them he was always busy and changed the subject. I thought I saw a quick eye exchange between Mr. and Mrs. Lamont, but they never brought up my dad again.

Saturdays were spent at Sharon's from 10-3. I could tell now that Sharon was living in her store. I noticed a tiny refrigerator and a microwave set up on a table in the corner next to the folded-up bed. The bathroom had towels, and I could tell by the wet shower door, that she had been using it regularly. I wondered what was going on but said nothing. Sharon seemed her happy self, and if she wanted to live in her store, I guess she could.

The Saturday after Leo's parents' party, Mr. Cooper came in and asked Sharon if she wanted to go to dinner. I think they have been going out a lot since then, but I don't ask her anything. If she wanted to tell me, she would.

Every Saturday around 3:00, Leo waltzes into Sharon's Riches, and we walk to the beach. I didn't want to swim by Jewel's and Charlotte's estates anymore, so we started swimming north towards the pier. There were more people that direction and the pier always had a mixture of locals fishing and tourists wandering. Leo and I started walking the pier, checking out who was catching what fish, before swimming back to our spot and then walking back to Leo's house.

And every Saturday night, as I boarded the city bus at 6:00 to return home, I saw Mr. Cooper pull his car up to the side of the road and hand a sandwich to the homeless man with the burgundy hoodie and Walmart shopping cart, and I would think, I'm so glad Sharon is dating him. He is a nice man.

Chapter Fifty-eight

Leo's birthday was December 15th, and his mom threw a party for our group: Dexter, Fish, Kendall, Macy, a new friend from our building program named Dushon, and me. It was on a Friday, and we all walked together to Leo's after school. His mom had set up a volleyball net in the backyard, and we played while Mr. Lamont grilled hamburgers and hot dogs.

We all crowded around an outdoor table and ate and laughed and when Mrs. Lamont brought out the cake with seventeen candles on it, we all sang, including Jenny and Christopher who had been running around the yard.

"Have you guys studied for midterms yet?" asked Kendall.

Dexter said, "No, don't talk about it. I'm having too much fun. I am studying all day tomorrow and Sunday."

"Me, too," said Macy. And we all agreed it was going to be a study weekend so better have fun tonight.

Dexter added, "The only class I don't have a midterm in is Mr. Cooper's class. He is the best."

Leo laughed, "Yea, because he is dating Vivian's boss, and he doesn't want to grade anything."

Dexter said, "Really? Cool. I'm glad. He deserves to be happy after what he has been through."

"What happened to him?" Kendall asked.

"My mom is a real estate agent and she told me that Mr. Cooper used to be the number one luxury home builder in all of Portofino. He won all kinds of awards and everything. Then this really rich woman hired him to remodel her estate and drove him out of business. Mom said she kept making demand after demand and Mr. Cooper is so nice, he kept wanting to please her and nothing was ever good enough. She blamed him for every little thing and then sued him when he said he couldn't work on her project anymore. I guess she had major connections and won the lawsuit. It ruined him and he lost his building license. Then his wife left him."

I thought of that sweet man who takes a sandwich and drink to the homeless guy everyday –even Saturdays—and I got madder and madder. I couldn't stand listening to any more of this story. I was so enraged. Without thinking I blurted out, *"WHAT IS*

WRONG WITH PEOPLE? WHY WOULD SOMEONE SUE HIM? WHY WOULD HIS WIFE LEAVE HIM? ARE PEOPLE THAT SHALLOW? DO PEOPLE ONLY THINK ABOUT THEMSELVES? THINGS HAPPEN IN LIFE. SOMETIMES BAD THINGS. IT DOESN'T MEAN YOU JUST SUE SOMEONE. IT DOESN'T MEAN YOU JUST QUIT ON SOMEONE. WHY ARE PEOPLE SO CRUEL?" I didn't realize that tears were streaming down my face until one dropped on the table. Startled, I jumped up and ran to the bathroom.

After a few minutes, I heard, "Viv, are you OK?" Leo said calmly while knocking softly.

I opened the door and said, "Yea. I'm sorry. I didn't mean to ruin your party."

"You didn't ruin my party. I am having a great time. But I want to know if you are doing OK. Is there anything you want to talk about?" His hand touched my face.

I looked into his amazingly kind, blue eyes and suddenly wanted to tell him everything. About my dad getting sued and slipping into depression. About my mom trying to keep it together, but then giving up and leaving. About my dad giving up and leaving. About the electricity turning off. About the water turning off. About the phone turning off. About having to bathe and go to the bathroom in the bushes. About roaches crawling all over me in the cafeteria. About selling all of mom and dad's stuff to pay the bills and buy food. About stealing from Jewel to pay off the homeowner's dues so I didn't get evicted. I wanted to tell him everything. But I couldn't. I liked things the way they were right now. I couldn't risk losing this. Leo and his family made me feel loved and losing that would destroy me.

So, I said, "Everything is fine. It just made me mad. I see Mr. Cooper always feeding that homeless man every day when I am on the bus going home from school. He even feeds him on Saturday. He didn't deserve to lose his license. He didn't deserve losing his wife."

Leo gave me a hug and gently kissed me and looked straight into my eyes, "I love you."

Our eyes were locked. "I love you, too."

We kissed, soft and sweet.

"Look, if those things hadn't happened to Mr. Cooper, he wouldn't be our teacher and he wouldn't be dating Sharon. Dexter is right. Mr. Cooper has been super happy lately. This is his story. As awful as those things were that happened to him, look what is happening now. Good things. Things that never would have happened if the bad things hadn't."

The more he talked, the more I loved him.

Then he whispered, "Let's go enjoy the good things."

G. Keller

Chapter Fifty-nine

It was just starting to get light out when Leo crept into Macy and Jenny's room and tapped me on my back while I slept on the makeshift floor-bed.

"Come on, we are going to the beach," he whispered.

"Now?" I staggered up.

"Yea, you have to go home early today to study, so I want to go swim with you before you leave."

I loved the idea and quietly reached into my bag for my swimsuit. After quickly changing clothes, I emerged from the bathroom and joined Leo in the kitchen. Leo wrote a note for the sleeping house and left it on the table as we silently exited without waking anyone.

The beach was cool and calm and by the time we got there, the sky and water were a color wheel of blue.

We sunk into the chilly December waters, and Leo kissed me softly at first, but his desire grew. And so did mine.

We couldn't stop touching each other and kissing each other until he pulled away, and we both listened to our heavy breathing with our foreheads touching.

"Let's go out to the island again," he whispered.

"I don't know. We need to study," I said, but I wanted to in the worst way.

"This is our last chance to go out there until next spring. My mom said the prince is coming next weekend with his new wife. She has been getting the place ready for their return. Come on. One last time."

Without answering, I began swimming to the island. Smooth, gliding motions with Leo by my side. When we reached the tiny beach, we flopped on our backs, breathing heavily. "You know what I really want to do?"

"What?" he said kissing my neck.

"Swim in that amazing pool."

Leo and I both looked around. It was still early. No boats. No people on the beach. "Just a couple of laps," I whispered.

He grabbed my hand, and we swam the short distance to the rocky barrier and climbed to the pool deck. "Come on," he said.

We both gingerly tip toed into the pool, holding hands the entire time. I couldn't believe this swimming pool. Water flowed over the far side like a gentle waterfall cascading into the ocean.

"They call this an infinity pool. Because the water looks like it goes on forever. My mom told me. Several of her clients have expensive pools like this one."

I didn't care if I ever lived in a magnificent mansion, but this pool was a different story. I would love to have this pool. I sunk under the water, held my breath, and swam the entire length, forgetting everything except the smooth, weightless drag of fresh water. When I popped up at the deep end of the pool, Leo was right there, so close, looking straight into my eyes with desire.

I reached for his hand underwater while holding onto the edge with my other. We kissed again and again, gaining urgency. I hadn't known what a kiss was supposed to feel like before Leo, because when I was forced to kiss Langston in the closet at Brianna's house, that is exactly what it felt like – forced….and fake. I hadn't known what to do with my lips or mouth or hands and Langston was irritated with me because of it.

But with Leo, I instinctively knew what to do. We swam halfway back to the shallow end, finding a spot where we both could stand. My hands lightly touched his smooth shoulders and then naturally slid down his arms and then over to his chest and around to the small of his back. My lips kissed his mouth in a perfect rhythm of gentleness and urgency, like the swell of the ocean waves, with moments of eye locking lust and passion. How did my body know exactly what to do? There, in that endless pool of water, my love for Leo made me feel less lost and less lonely.

"I like the name of this pool," he whispered between kisses. "Infinity. That is my love for you. Infinity."

I wanted to sink into Leo forever and forget everything else in my life. I pulled him so close to me, pressing my body into his. He started to pull away, but I wouldn't let him. I didn't want to let go of him, of this moment.

He took control this time and grabbed my arms, gently but also firmly, letting me know he was going to end this escalating emotional exchange. He pulled back, unlocking our kiss.

"Slow down, Viv, you are killing me here," he whispered with a slight smile. "I want you in the worst way, but not now. Not here."

"Why not? This is perfect. The infinity pool. Just us." I tried pulling him closer.

"No, I promised my mom I wouldn't do this. She told me that if I really was falling in love with you, I would respect you and wait," Leo said with our foreheads touching.

I was disappointed, but I lingered on the word love.

He truly loved me.

Suddenly there was a noise coming from the house. Startled, Leo and I jumped out of the pool, scurrying to the nearest bush and crouching down. The French doors flew open, and a woman walked out with a white flowing dress and a white scarf wrapped around her head and face. She had large black sunglasses on and walked straight out to the very point of the pool deck, staring out to sea.

Leo and I froze. My heart was pounding with the fear of getting caught. She slowly unwrapped the white scarf to reveal her long silky brown hair. Her back was to us, and I could tell she was breathing in the view.

"Come on, let's go," Leo whispered.

I started to follow him and then something caught my eye, and I looked at the woman again. She turned so that I saw her profile. That jaw. That nose. I studied her body.

I knew that body.

I froze again.

Leo kept tapping me to come on and hurry, finally pulling me away.

The hair was different but everything else was Mom.

Chapter Sixty

I walked back to Leo's house in a daze.

"Is everything ok?"

I didn't want to alarm him.

"No, I just feel faint again. I need water."

This pacified him and as soon as we got to his house, I drank a tall glass of water.

"I really have to go study. I am starting to worry about my math midterm. You don't need to walk me to the bus."

Sensing a slightly bewildered expression on Leo's face, I refused to make eye contact. I kissed him on the cheek quickly and raced out the door.

Settled in the bus seat with my backpack in my lap, I let out a long sigh. What just happened? Did I really see what I thought I saw at the prince's palace? I had thought many times about the day I saw mom board that jet with that old man. Was that the prince she was with that day? I didn't really pay attention to him other than he looked old. Her hair was her usual blonde, and I saw her face plain that day. I knew it was her. But this woman had brown hair. Maybe I was mistaken.

Looking out the window, I saw that same bum pushing his Walmart cart. How could this town have two completely different worlds.... minutes away from each other? How can one person spend millions on a house they lived in two months a year or less, when another person is hoping a schoolteacher gives them a sandwich each day? How could a woman care so much about money that she would leave her family penniless to starve? Like that bum. How did he get to the point where he was pushing a cart filled with a few belongings, begging for food?

I kept recreating the woman I saw today in my head. Her brown hair was not blonde like my mom's. She had on large sunglasses. Maybe I was mistaken. Maybe it was a mirage. Maybe my loneliness was causing my mind to play tricks on me. Maybe I had been dehydrated and delusional. But the way she stood with her chin slightly raised in arrogance, her square jawline, her body frame, all was identical to mom. I knew mom's slightest movements. And although her walk had acquired an angry edge to it in the last two years, I knew the angle of her neck and chin. I knew the way she lifted her hand to touch her hair – no matter the color of it. And I knew the casual confidence having money and stature gave her and that is what I saw today. The old mom. The mom before the incident. The relaxed mom. The mom with money.

If it was her, how could she just cut me off like this? Why not just divorce dad and marry this prince guy and keep me in her life? Why the reinvention? New hair? New name probably? New life? It didn't make sense. Maybe this prince kidnapped her. Maybe he was so grief stricken about losing his wife, he saw my mom and forced her to be with him. As awful as that played out in my head, I liked it better than she just didn't want me anymore. But she looked so relaxed and elegant, not like someone who was being held against their will.

If the woman I saw today was the prince's new wife, my mom, how could she marry someone else if she wasn't divorced from dad? Did she make up a new identity? She did leave her driver's license and social security card behind. But why? Was money so important that you not only left your husband and child, but you invented a whole new you. New name? New history? New future?

Was she that void of human compassion? Didn't she love me at all? I had been thinking lately that she had died in a horrible accident on her way back to me. And as horrible as that was, that morbid fantasy included her love for me. Was it better that she was dead and still wanted me as her daughter? Or alive with the reality of complete rejection.

Dead. Dead, knowing she loved me, was better.

I could understand her rejecting dad. He had become pathetic on the sofa. And she had tried. For two and a half years she tried. Didn't she? Didn't she try? She kept saying she was trying, but maybe she was really the problem? Maybe she was the cause of Dad not getting up and moving on? Her constant badgering. Her constant complaining. Her constant blaming. Her constant spending. Maybe she thought she was trying, but she wasn't.

But me? I am her daughter. I am her blood. Is money that intoxicating that you could calculate an elaborate lie and cut off your only daughter? Never see her again in exchange for a palace or palaces? Pretend you are a completely different person so you can drive a fancy car? Eat fancy food? Travel to fancy places?

It couldn't be her. She couldn't do that to me. She couldn't – could she?

I had to go out there again. I had to see if it was her.

I had to know.

And if it was her, I had to ask her – why?

Chapter Sixty-one

Wednesday, December 20th, was the last day of the semester. Mr. Cooper was the only teacher not giving a midterm, so he decided to start the new quarter's classwork early. The title of the second semester class was Drafting II and he said he wanted to get the section on laws of building over with, so we could have fun creating house designs beginning in January. Therefore, we all sat through a long and boring power point on building laws.

I was half listening because my obsession with the woman I saw at the pointe palace had taken up every space in my head. I was plotting how I was going to swim out there tomorrow, alone, and see if it was her. But what would I do if I found her? What would I say? I wanted to scream at her and blow her cover. Let her new prince husband know she was a fraud. But why?

Force her to come live with me again – force her to be my mother? How can you force someone to love you?

You can't.

If she didn't want me as a daughter, what could I do?

Mr. Cooper was droning on about laws I cared nothing about, nor did anyone else. The class was falling asleep in the dark room, sleep deprived from pulling all-nighters studying for other class midterms. Then I heard something that caught my attention.

"In order to obtain the title of a house, you must have it legally deeded over to you," Mr. Cooper seemed as bored as everyone else.

I was suddenly interested. My mission to fix the house and sell it always held one major problem that I was not facing – I didn't legally own the house. Deep down I knew I couldn't sell it without mom or dad. I think I believed one of them would return by the time I had it fixed, but now I realized that may never happen. And if I wanted to pay back Jewel for all the money I stole, I had to sell it.

"How do you do that Mr. Cooper?" I suddenly had an idea.

"Well, you can go to a lawyer and have them draw up the papers for the owner to sign over the title or you can get the forms from the courthouse," said Mr. Cooper.

I heard nothing else after that. I waited for class to end and everyone to leave, so I could ask Mr. Cooper a question. I remembered asking my mom once why they didn't just sell the house—even if it was unfinished—and buy a small house. She said dad refused. He wouldn't take a loss on the house. Mom couldn't sell it without both of them agreeing. I wanted to ask Mr. Cooper if it was legal to sell the house if one person abandoned the other, but I didn't want to give away my situation.

"Mr. Cooper, can a parent give the deed of a house to a child?"

"Yes, there is something called a quick claim deed. This is how family members usually transfer a deed to a property. Does that answer your question?"

"Yes, thank you." I had so many questions I wanted to ask, but feared I would raise further suspicion if I continued this topic. "I'm just really interested in real estate law. I find it fascinating."

Mr. Cooper had a quizzical smirk on his face, and I left before he could ask me anything that might lead him to wonder more. I decided to do the rest of my research on getting the deed to my house from the internet at home, but for now, I was filled with excitement at the possibility that I could own the house, my house. The house I didn't abandon.

My mind was racing with plans to take over ownership. I suddenly knew exactly what I would say to the woman in the palace, the woman who had to be my mother. I wouldn't beg her return. I wouldn't beg for her love. I wouldn't beg her for anything.

I would just ask for one thing. One thing that I deserved.

The title of the house.

Who stayed when things got hard?

Me.

Who figured out how to pay the electricity bill? The water bill? The phone bill?

Me. Me. Me.

Who had to break into a house and steal money that YOU owed to save the house?

Me.

I deserved the title to the house, and I was going to get it.

Chapter Sixty-two

I was so engrossed in my plan that I didn't look for Leo after school and marched straight for my bus ride home, thinking about how I was going to go to the courthouse tomorrow and how I was going to swim out to the prince's palace with the papers for mom to sign – *if t*hat woman really was my mom. I started to rehearse dialogue exchanges with her like 'How could you leave me like that?' and 'You selfish uncaring human.' And 'I hate you' and 'You owe me.'

I was so inside my head that I didn't even hear Leo calling my name until I was seated on my empty bus. As we pulled away from the curb, I looked out and saw him running towards the bus saying in a fading distance 'Hold on.' I saw a look in his eyes that I didn't recognize. Hurt? Had I hurt him? I couldn't stand the thought of hurting him.

I waved.

My phone instantly binged.

Leo texted, "What happened to you today? You seemed mad at me."

"I'm not mad. Just exhausted from exams," I texted back. "I'll call you tonight," I added.

"K."

Why would he think I was mad at him? He was perfect in every way. I loved how easy he was to be around. I loved how he was so comfortable in his own skin. I loved how he knew exactly what he was going to do with his life. I loved his family. I loved his unpretentiousness. I loved the way he looked at me, the way he kissed me, the way he talked to me and respected me. I loved him so much it hurt.

But I couldn't love him the way he truly deserved until I got myself out of this mess I was in. I couldn't drag him into my complicated world. He has such a perfect life. How would it look if his dad – a police officer--- found out his son was in love with a thief? And not a petty thief, although that would be horrible too, but a grand thief, a $35,000 thief? What have I done getting involved with such a nice person when what I've done is so despicable?

I knew what I had to do. I had to get out of this mess I was in before going any further in a relationship with Leo. I had to tell him tonight that I needed space. As much as I didn't want to do it, as much as he was the only good thing in my life, I had to take a break from him for a while until I figured out how to get the title of my house and sell it and then pay back Jewel. How could I have let things get this far? How could I fall in love with Leo when my life was such a lie? I wanted so much to be normal. To have a normal life. And Leo and his family were normal and wonderful, and I wanted to pretend my life wasn't what it was: A train wreck. I had to get my life in order. Then I would be worthy of being Leo's girlfriend.

I had to tell him I needed space. Even though I didn't want it. He couldn't know about me. Not yet. Not until I got myself in a better situation.

The bus had come to a stop, and I looked up from my phone to see why. The traffic was stagnant, and I could see there was a jam ahead. I guess the last day of school before winter break provoked extra traffic. I glanced around. We hadn't gotten far. In fact, we were still in front of the school, and I could see Mr. Cooper walking up the sidewalk with his usual sandwich for the homeless man. But the homeless man was nowhere. Mr. Cooper looked around trying to find him.

He looked up at the bus and saw me in it and waved. I waved back. What a nice human Mr. Cooper was, taking the time to feed that man every day. I was glad Sharon was dating him. I hope she continued. I didn't know why she had been sleeping in her store, but maybe if things go well, she will marry him.

Then I thought of Leo and how much I loved him. I wanted to be with him forever. I rushed him when we were in the infinity pool. Running my hands all over his body, urging him on, feeling his desire grow, wanting to get lost in the intensity of what I was feeling, to forget everything else going on, to pretend I was just a normal girl madly in love and never wanting the feeling to end. I wanted to skip over this part of my life and jump right into adulthood. I pushed him, and I shouldn't have. What did he think of me now? I could have ruined everything with him. He had pulled away and told me to stop. Not yet he had said. Slow down he had said. I love you, he had said.

Then the sudden noise, hiding in the bushes, watching the woman walk out on the pool deck in her white flowing gown, like a princess in a palace, her head turning, reality slapping my face like a stormy wave. Could that have been mom?

***

That night I lay in bed listening to the Rolling Stones *You Can't Always Get What You Want* with just the light of my phone adding a narrow, shallow field of vision and casting a blurred, vague shadow against the wall. I was putting off calling Leo. I didn't want to have that conversation. He had already left me two voicemails and three texts, but that was three hours ago, and now I knew he was waiting for me.

What could I say without hurting him? It was 11:49, almost midnight, but I knew he was still up and waiting for me. Probably wondering why I haven't called.

A roach crawled along the wall next to my bed. I shined the little phone flashlight at him. He was worried and started to scurry. Roach Girl. It seemed like forever ago that I was in the cafeteria of Beachside Middle School with roaches crawling all over me and kids laughing and pointing and taking pictures of me. The day I met Leo for the first time. He knew nothing about Roach Girl and all my problems.

How did I deserve Leo? Roach girl used a bush for a bathroom. Roach Girl stole money to pay her bills....Leo can't be involved with me. He deserves better than Roach Girl. Why had I let things get this far with him?

I didn't know how to tell him I couldn't see him for a while.

I didn't want to make that call.

So, I didn't.

Chapter Sixty-three

I put together the same ritual as when I stole from Jewel: expensive bathing suit, shorts, t-shirt cover up, flip flops and a waterproof backpack I found at Target in the camping section to hold the documents I needed mom to sign, so I could be owner of the house. I also put a water bottle in the backpack, so I wouldn't get dehydrated. I couldn't get sick on this journey.

When I walked out of Royal Palm Estates and passed Winston at the guard gate, a car was pulling through the entrance, and a woman rolled down her window to say hi to Winston, handing him a treat of some sort. I recognized the woman as the chef at the clubhouse that had me taste her muffins last summer when I hadn't had anything good to eat in so long. I remembered what a great cook she was.

She spotted me walking out the exit side of the guardhouse and called for me, "Hey."

I heard Winston say something to her and she shouted again, "Vivian. I have another new muffin recipe I want you to try."

The last thing I wanted right now was a muffin, and I couldn't run it back to the house because I would be late for the bus.

As politely as I could, I yelled back, "No thank you, I'm meeting a friend."

"Here take one to your friend, too. I need to know if people like them. I am experimenting with fresh ingredients in the muffins. I won't tell you what they are until you tell me whether you like them or not."

She wasn't going to take no for an answer, and I needed to hurry. I grabbed two muffins from her, and she handed me a huge napkin. I quickly wrapped them up and opened my backpack and shoved them into an inner zipped pouch.

"Thank you," and I smiled politely.

I had to run to catch the bus to the south side of town, where the courthouse was located.

It took several people and a couple of lines at the courthouse to get the proper papers. I had to tell two different ladies I was getting the papers for my sick mother. Once I finally had them, I took another bus back to the stop next to Sharon's Riches and then headed straight to the beach.

My heart was racing as soon as I got to the sandy shoreline, and I looked out at the palace on the peninsula. I rolled up my shorts, t-shirt and flip flops and stuffed them into the waterproof backpack with the documents. I pulled out the muffins and realized I hadn't eaten today – too nervous— so I decided I better eat one for strength. I was going to throw the other one away but decided to wrap it up in a napkin the lady had given me and put it back into the inner zippered pouch.

I had to go now.

I waded out into the cool water and sunk below the surface with the backpack in my hand. Swimming out to the small island was harder with the backpack, but with my expert swimming skills, I managed to get there. Once on the shore, I sat to catch my breath. It felt strange and vacant and lonely to be here without Leo. Leo. I longed for him to be here with me right now. To face this woman together. To tell him everything about me. To release the burden of lies I carried. To have him hold me and tell me he would always be there for me. To hear him say he would never leave me.

I shook off thinking of Leo and waded knee high through a narrow waterway and climbed up the rocky edge to the pool deck area. I walked right up in plain view but didn't see anyone. I walked around the perimeter of the house, stopping briefly to throw on a t-shirt, shorts, and flip flops. On the second walk around, I heard some activity coming from the front of the house in the circular driveway. I saw the woman who had to be my mother getting into a fancy black car and start to drive away.

I walked up to a man still standing in the driveway and said, "Where is she going?"

"Who are you?" The man looked baffled at my presence.

Suddenly startled by the realization that I just spoke that out loud and not in my head, I stuttered, "family."

"Where did you come from?" The man was irritated now, but so was I.

"Where is she going?" I shouted the question loudly.

"The airport," the man said.

"Take me there, NOW!"

There was another vehicle parked in the circular driveway and I ran to it, opening the passenger door that was unlocked. The man pulled keys out of his pocket and reluctantly got in the driver seat.

I could tell by the perplexed look on his face that he wasn't sure he should be taking orders from a stranger, but orders were part of his job….and I hardly looked like a criminal, standing there in damp clothes over a wet bathing suit. I looked like I could be family. He ultimately decided to take me to the airport and let the drama unfold there.

"Faster," I yelled, suddenly worried I was going to miss my opportunity to catch mom before she left again for God knows how long. And I needed her to sign these papers. If she wanted out of my life, fine, but she owes me big. She owes me the right to the house she left me in—alone—to fend for myself.

The car screeched to a halt in front of the executive airport where all the private jets were parked. The one where I saw a blonde mom months ago. The one across the busy road where The Priceless Pawn and LWTHS called home. The one a few blocks from Leo and Sharon's Riches. The one where a brunette mom was about to board her own private plane, again.

I flew out of the car and ran as fast as I could through security when I saw her climbing the steps to the plane.

"STOP!" shouted a security guard.

I didn't listen to his frighteningly loud command.

"STOP now. This is a felony!"

"MOOOOOM!" I screamed so loud that the residue of those three letters lingered in the air like a sad canyon echo. Three letters shouted with such passion and fury and sorrow and uncontrolled longing that everyone stopped.

The security guard. The man who drove me here. And a few new bystanders.

And the woman.

She was wearing a beautiful yellow brocade dress, high-heeled wedge sandals, pearl necklace, and carried an oversized expensive handbag. It had to be mother.

She pulled off her large black sunglasses and there standing before me, bewildered, was a woman I suddenly didn't recognize at all.

This was not my mother.

I was breathing hard. Oh God, what have I done? I was so sure it was her I hadn't considered what I would do if it wasn't.

I heard the faint police siren in the distance coming closer. I panicked.

I looked at the entrance, and it was blocked with security and other people standing there watching the freak show.

I looked over at the loops of barbed wire topping the chain link fence. I couldn't let them get me. Everything would come out. That I was living alone. That I had stolen money to pay bills. Leo would hate me for lying and stealing and I would never see him again. I couldn't let them arrest me.

Because of all the months of practice hurdling the iron gate to mom's courtyard, I ditched my flip-flops and managed my way over the fence, effortlessly, before security knew what was happening. The pain I felt when I grabbed the barbed wire didn't matter. I just had to get out of there before the police came. Like Spiderman, I popped up instantly and disappeared across Airport Road, down the street of my school. I ran past the sign that read 'Lorenzo Williams Technical High School' into the neighborhood of run-down houses with three and four cars and trucks parked in driveways. I was thankful for the overstuffed garages because it made my disappearance easier. I slipped between a few junky yards and exited down an alley and ran until houses ended and a dense forest of spindly pine trees and thick palmetto scrub brush began.

The scrub brush was so wild, I had a hard time running through it, especially without shoes. Then I saw a slightly worn-down path. Once on it, I ran and ran and ran until I thought I would pass out and stopped to listen. I could still hear the police sirens, but they seemed far away.

This was it. My secret was about to be discovered. No more hiding behind the brick wall of

Royal Palm Estates. No more Friday nights at the Lamonts. No more beach days with Leo. No more Sharon's Riches. No more fantasies of fixing my house. Foster care here I come. Or maybe worse, juvenile detention or prison.

I looked down and saw scratches all over my legs and my hands and feet were bleeding badly from the barbed wire. I started walking a little further and then stopped abruptly. There was the Walmart shopping cart full of stuff. The bum. The one that Mr. Cooper fed every day.

I looked around, scared. What would he do if he found me out here alone? I didn't see him. I crept quietly, still hearing distant sirens looking for me. Maybe he was nice. Maybe he would hide me until they gave up looking. Where was he? My eyes darted desperately up and down the dirt path. Nothing.

Then I saw him crouched in a fetal position under a small tree in the shade. His dirty, shabby burgundy hoodie covered him up completely, and he seemed to melt into the thicket, disappearing from sight, like a wild animal hiding from predators. I slowly walked closer, not wanting to startle him out of his slumber. He might have a gun or knife ready to kill. After all, it would be scary living out here in wild Florida, where panthers, bears, wolves and probably other unseemly people, bucking society for criminal reasons, lived. Like me. Sirens searching for my whereabouts, ready to cuff me and take me down to the station for a police drilling that would undoubtedly discover my thieving existence?

"Excuse me," I said softly.

No response.

I cleared my throat, "Excuse me," I said a little louder.

Nothing. Was he dead? I remembered Mr. Cooper looking for him yesterday and he wasn't there for his usual sandwich. Maybe he had gotten really sick.

I went closer and saw his chest moving up and down slightly under the zippered hoodie. He wasn't dead. I couldn't see his face because the hood covered it up. But I could see his long scraggly beard cascading to the ground, giving ants and roaches a place to explore.

Suddenly, a strange feeling shot through my body. I scrutinized him as I slowly moved closer, eyeing every detail like I had not done before. A skeleton of a man lay limp beneath the worn-out clothes. Then I froze. His shoes. Holey, dirty, and worn until almost unrecognizable, but once expensive Cole Hahn loafers.

No.

No.

My heart raced.

His beard was longer than I remember. It couldn't be. An image of a cartoonish skeleton of a man with an overgrown beard passed out on the sofa flashed in my head.

I knelt down slowly and whispered, "Daddy?"

Chapter Sixty-four

He opened his bleary eyes trying to focus. Then grunted and closed them back up. His mouth had formed a white crust, and I suddenly panicked that he was dying. All these months without him. All these months seeing him on the street and not even knowing it was him. All these months thinking he had left home for a better life. After all these months, I finally found him, and now I was afraid I might lose him.

Slipping out of my backpack, I unzipped the outer and then inner compartment with crust covered, bloody hands and found my water bottle and the muffin I thankfully saved. I lifted his head, "Daddy, it's me, Vivian. You have to drink something daddy, please."

He lifted his head again and tried opening his eyes. I held the water bottle to his lips.

"Just take a little sip. Please," I pleaded, tears sliding down my face.

I broke off a bit of the smashed muffin and forced it into his mouth. The crumbs fell to the ground, but his lips began moving to taste it. I broke off another bit, and he sort of ate it. I held the water again and he drank a sip.

I held him then, crying harder and harder. "Daddy, I found you."

I tried to lift him up a little and felt dizzy. I took a tiny sip of water myself to gain some strength. My head started to spin, and my mouth felt like cotton. How was I going to get us both out of here? Maybe if we just rest a bit and wait a while, I can get us back to the bus stop and then home. My head felt dizzier, and I took another short sip and bite of muffin. I forced more liquid and nourishment down dad's mouth.

His eyes opened, but they looked delirious, and I could tell he didn't recognize me. He didn't speak or make eye contact at all. In fact, he seemed confused and lost.

"Shhh, you don't have to say anything, dad." I gently rested his head back down on the pile of dead foliage. I put one arm around his anorexic body and rested my head on his shoulder. "I'm here now, dad. It's Vivian. I'm here."

I was so shocked and engrossed in helping my dad that I hadn't been paying attention to the louder police siren and then the abrupt silence. I didn't hear people forging through the brush. I didn't hear murmured worried whispers. I didn't hear the familiar voice gently calling my name. Until finally, I did hear.

"Vivian......Vivian?" I couldn't look up for fear of losing my dad again. I didn't realize I was crying now. I was clinging to him so tightly and sobbing so loudly that my whole body heaved up and down.

A gentle, familiar touch found my shoulder. I managed to look up.

Leo was kneeling next to me with confusion etched on his face. Behind him were his dad in uniform, Sharon, and Mr. Cooper.

Mr. Cooper knelt down too. "Do you know him, Vivian?"

I couldn't stop my tears and nodded yes and muffled out a garbled,

"He's my dad."

Afterward

Mr. Cooper took my dad into his home for the two-week holiday vacation. He had experience with helping alcoholics and said when I found Dad, he was going through stage two or three of the withdrawal process which can include confusion, hallucinations, fever and even death. Given the harsh living circumstances he had been in, Mr. Cooper said he would have died if I hadn't found him.

Mr. Cooper bought my dad the study books for taking the teacher's exam. He told dad they needed medical teachers at LWTHS. He also gave my dad the study books for getting his contractor's license. Apparently, it was a secret passion he and Mr. Cooper bonded over while he was helping dad recover.

Sharon moved in with me-- until dad got better, she said.

I loved having her with me those weeks that dad recovered. She treated me like a daughter she never had. We Christmas shopped for everyone and cooked on the camper's kitchen – which she said was better than her usual takeout.

She shared with me how she had been living in her dad's condo after he died but couldn't afford it anymore. She sold it but made no money on it because her dad had taken out a large loan a few years ago to pay medical bills. She was just living in her shop until she could find a place. She told me her business was doing much better thanks to me, and she would be looking for a place to live soon.

We celebrated Christmas a few days late with Leo and his family, Mr. Cooper, Sharon, dad, and me. After everyone gorged on the amazing turkey and mashed potatoes and gravy and green beans and casseroles and cranberry and laughter, Leo took my hand and pulled me away from the crowded kitchen to the backyard, where the crisp night air sparkled with strung twinkle lights and echoed complete quiet.

"I have something for you," he said looking deep into my eyes with the calmest smile, then sliding one arm around my waist pulling me close.

He pulled out a small box from his pocket with his free hand.

"What is this?" I asked, surprised.

"I hope you don't mind. It made me think of you. You love the beach and swim like a fish, and I found it at the Priceless Pawn – your favorite store. When you first told me that you were obsessed with shopping there, I started going, hoping to see you, but I never did. When I found this, I told Roy that it was for you, although he seems to think your name is Victoria. Anyway, he gave me a great deal. I hope you like it."

I stepped back a little and took the box from him. It was a beautiful pale gold charm bracelet with only one charm, a dolphin with a sapphire eye.

"I love it," I said and kissed him. "I have something for you, too. Wait here." I dashed back to the house and returned with a shirt-sized white box with a gold bow.

Leo started to untie the bow, and I said, "Sharon doesn't really take in men's clothing and what she does take is usually very high-end stuff. So, when someone brought this in, I quickly snatched it."

Leo pulled out a turquoise blue T-shirt with a large retro tie-dyed peace sign on it. He immediately whipped off his shirt and pulled it over his head and smiled. "I love it."

"It made me think of you because ever since that first day I met you in the media center, you have brought me peace."

He pulled me back close to him, and we stood under the twinkle lights and kissed.

***

One year after my parents walked out on me, the unfinished mansion in Royal Palm Estates was not only finished but won first place in a 'Best Remodels' competition put on by the Portofino Homebuilder's Association. Construction and building students from LWTHS (including Leo and me) helped Mr. Cooper and my dad design and finish a spectacular home.

It sold for $2.2 million dollars.

First, we paid back Jewel and her husband. After dad was found, I confessed my entire story. Sharon and Leo's dad went straight to Jewel and her husband with the truth. As it turned out, my dad had performed eye surgery years ago on Jewel's husband, and he loved my dad and found the whole situation sad and unfortunate. Jewel and her husband not only accepted the payback deal, but they also wanted to set up special scholarship funds for the students at LWTHS.

Second, we bought three small houses in Leo's neighborhood, two to fix up and sell and one to fix up and live in. Mr. Cooper also bought a fixer-upper for him and Sharon, who had gotten engaged. My dad and Mr. Cooper formed their own construction company, specializing in remodeling with the goal of making Leo's neighborhood look refreshed and pretty—like Leo's house.

Third, my dad let me pick the name of the company. I chose RG Construction. I told everyone it stood for Real Good Construction…they laughed at the bluntness of it, but inside I knew what it really stood for: Roach Girl Construction, an indestructible building company.

As for my mom, she never returned. After mistaking that woman from the point palace for my mom, I began to question whether the woman from last year that boarded that jet was just an illusion, too. Regardless, mom was gone. And while my heart was almost completely full with dad back and Leo in my life, there was a void…… a hole in my heart where her love used to be.

Roach Girl origin trilogy two

Where did Vivian's mother go? Was it simply that she wanted a new life or was there more to her departure than Vivian realized…...?

About the Author

Gina Keller is a middle school English teacher and writer originally from Aberdeen, South Dakota. She has a bachelor's degree in psychology and early childhood education from North Carolina State University. After graduating, she moved to Orlando, Florida where she began her education career. While teaching, Keller fell in love with literature and writing. Having been a member of SCBWI, Keller has attended national writing conferences in Los Angeles, New York, and Miami, where she began to grow as a writer. She moved with her husband to Naples, Florida, where they raised their family, and Keller continued teaching and writing. The idea for the Roach Girl origin trilogy came to Keller when she was teaching middle school in Naples. After moving back to Orlando, Keller finished the trilogy and is currently working on new writing projects. Roach Girl origin trilogy is her first published works.

About the Artist

Janelle Bell-Martin is a freelance illustrator working on book illustration, collectible designs, animation final line art and painting.

.